Prime Prey

KAENAR LANGFORD

What the critics are saying...

ഌ

JUDE'S CHOICE

4.5 Stars "Jude's Choice is a winning combination of futuristic fantasy and good old fashion eroticism. The characters have so much personality and sensuality that they jump off the pages in this story. As a reader, I can not wait for more from this highly talented author." ~ *Sensual EcataRomance Reviews*

ABSOLUTE TRUST

***Absolute Trust* won the 2008 Sensual Reviewer's Choice Award from Cata Network**

4.5 Blue Ribbons "ABSOLUTE TRUST is a wonderful read and I for one will be looking out for more from this series. The series so far in order of release are JUDE'S CHOICE and ABSOLUTE TRUST." ~ *Romance Junkies Reviews*

An Ellora's Cave Romantica Publication

www.ellorascave.com

Prime Prey

ISBN 9781419958748

Edited by Helen Woodall and Meghan Conrad.
Cover art by Syneca.

This book printed in the U.S.A. by Jasmine-Jade Enterprises, LLC.

Trade paperback Publication February 2009

PRIME PREY

ꕥ

JUDE'S CHOICE

Dedication

ജ

To my husband and sons – who do all they can to support my writing habit

To my friend Bea – who started it all with an ad in her bookstore

To my editor Helen Woodall – who is always there and who always encourages me

To my friends and colleagues – who never fail to make me feel like one in a million

Chapter One

ཙ

"So how long do you think this one will last?" Angelina asked Delia as they watched him rock back and forth, sweat coursing down his face. They could see how hard it was for him to hold on. The muscles in his shoulders were as taut as steel and his face was suffused from the exertion. He knew he wasn't going to be able to hang on much longer but he refused to let go. All the others had gone off too soon and he needed to show he could go the distance. Now he was furiously pumping up and down, trying to stay on, trying to keep the upper hand, so to speak. He probably had no idea what kind of a ride he was going to get until it was too late. He looked down but couldn't focus on the body below him, the images blurring as he heaved and bucked, trying desperately to stay on top.

"I still can't believe people would want an audience for this kind of thing!" Angelina said. "You'd think that they wouldn't want anyone to see them when they can't hold on any longer."

"It must be some kind of macho thing," Delia mused. "You know what I mean, Lina. Even if they blow too soon at least everyone gets to see what a stud they are for wanting to do it in front of us all."

"Too bad they don't have this kind of thing back home," Angelina continued, "but I guess if you hadn't screwed up that last mission to Antelika we wouldn't be taking this forced vacation to begin with."

"I don't know what you're complaining about," Delia shouted over the roar of the crowd as they cheered him on. "It's better than the stopover you organized last year on that pirate planet. At least we don't have to worry about getting seasick this time."

"How was I to know that the top two fighter pilots in the Wardelian League would be brought low by a lousy case of *mal de mer*? You'd think that two women who can thread a Pyrian cruiser through the eye of a needle could spend a week on a fake pirate ship without getting sick." Angelina shook her head, remembering the humiliation of a week at sea, on her back, without a man on top of her. What a waste of horizontal space, not to mention a three-day layover thrown away to boot! Groans from the crowd brought her back to the present just in time to see the latest entry thrown to the ground amid the hoots and hollers of the watchers. Turning to her captain, she asked, a sparkle in her eye, "By the way, what did you think of that big, gorgeous guy who was up just before this one? I was disappointed that he didn't last."

Happy to forget their ill-fated pirate holiday, Delia turned to her friend and said with a laugh, "I thought he would have been able to stay on longer. I would have liked to see him up close. When he peeled off his t-shirt and climbed on top I thought I was going to faint."

The two women had been friends since the academy when they had to prove to the young hotshot males that they were just as good. Being the only females in a group of testosterone-laden men set them together right from the day they arrived on Tenta as newbies. They had toughed it out and proven they were just as smart, just as wily and just as good at flying as any of the men. In fact, they had proven to be better. Delia couldn't wish for a better man at her back than this woman. As Angelina got up to get a better look as the latest guy got into position Delia had to laugh. For someone who hadn't wanted to take this forced holiday, Angelina certainly was interested. Maybe she just needed to get laid. Hell! Who didn't! Protecting the galaxy from evil didn't leave the two of them much time for a sex life and a one-night stand didn't appeal to Delia.

As Angelina forced her way to the front of the crowd, she looked back and gave Delia a naughty wink. She knew that look. Her friend had zeroed in on a likely candidate to warm her bunk for the night. What could she say? Lina was old enough to make her own choices. As she watched her friend melt into the crowd, she felt a light touch on the back of her neck as if someone had gently stroked a feather across her skin. She shivered in response but when she put her hand up to brush it away there was nothing there. She swiveled in her chair to look behind her but everyone was intent on the action and not a soul was nearby. Turning back, Delia watched in fascination as another one couldn't hold on any longer and fell in a heap, sweating and out of breath. The crowd moved forward, egging the next man on, encouraging him as he mounted.

Delia and Angelina had seen the ad in the local paper and had come to see what it was all about. Delia had no idea so many men would want to be thrown by a mechanical bull. It seemed crazy and a bit dangerous but the men lined up and took a turn getting thrown, one after another, onto their keister. But what else would you expect on a cowboy planet? Many of them were being pushed forward by their friends while others wanted to impress their girlfriend. How flopping at your girl's feet in an ignominious heap would impress her was beyond Delia's ken. The whole idea of planets devoted to fantasy themes had seemed so ludicrous when the Wardelian League had suggested the idea to the Galactic Council but the concept had proven to be hugely popular with new theme planets being added as quickly as the League could get them up and running. The list of planets was varied, that's for sure. As well as a pirate planet and the cowboy planet there were endless varieties of entertainment to be had. Some of the ideas that the Council had come up with had turned out to be hugely popular like the planet of unrequited love or damsels in distress. Delia thought it was bad enough living these things in your daily life without having them be a holiday destination.

She recalled some of the other planets listed on her compugram when she had to research a quick holiday for the two of them after that little incident on Antelika—a circus planet, a cop planet, a porn planet, a debutante planet, a famous cities of Old Earth planet. Some of them sounded intriguing but some of them just sounded silly. Delia had always thought that the Victorian planet sounded interesting. Any reading she'd done about that time on Earth made it seem like an interesting era, sexual repression on the surface but hidden debauchery underneath. Something wanton and naughty in her wanted to be a love slave or perhaps hold a man as her love slave.

She could think of one man in particular that she'd love to have at her mercy. She'd only had a brief glimpse of him once on Tristar 234 when she and Angelina had stopped there to refuel but that glimpse had fueled erotic fantasies for weeks to come. They'd been in the middle of a rescue mission to some backwater planet and out of time as always, yet she could remember every detail of the encounter. He had been hauling his latest "catch" to his cruiser and the stupid son of a bitch thought he'd make a last-ditch attempt to get away. The bounty hunter had hauled him up against his chest and whispered in his ear. The poor bastard had peed his pants and had never made another sound. Delia had been standing with her mouth open, watching the interplay, when he had whirled and looked right at her as if she'd just popped up on his radar screen. A wry smile had lit up his face as he had given her body a slow perusal, his hand around the felon's neck. As his eyes had traveled down her, Delia had sworn she could feel his hands touching her, pebbling her nipples, stroking her belly, nudging her clit. She had known he hadn't moved yet his touch was marking her, claiming her. Dragging his prisoner with him, he had moved over to stand in front of her. Delia had never backed down from a fight but the sheer animal power of this man had made her feel tiny and edgy as he had loomed over her. Leaning down, he had put out his tongue and licked below her ear. Delia had stood frozen as he had marked her.

"I'll find you," he had growled then had turned and disappeared into the rag tag crowd. Delia's face flooded with color as she remembered his smell, his face. Maybe she wasn't ready for the Victorian planet yet! She and Lina still had the rest of the week to spend on the cowboy planet and with chuck wagon races, barrel racing, trail rides and a rodeo it looked like their schedule was going to be busy. Too bad she couldn't work up any enthusiasm for the activities. Wardelian scientists had managed to reproduce as much as they could of the cowboy world from twenty-first-century Earth right down to horses and Brahma bulls but she wasn't a landlocked woman. Her link was to the sky. Perhaps it was because her years as a Pyrian fighter had allowed her to see so much of the galaxy that the sky was her home. Maybe she just needed to get out of here and get some air or get laid!

Laying her right hand up and across her breast, Delia tapped the tiny communicator to get in touch with Lina. Her ears were filled with the sounds of gasping and groaning, a sure sign that her navigator had succeeded in her quest.

"Sorry to interrupt," she whispered, "but I'm headed back to the cabin for the night." For a second she thought that Lina wouldn't answer then she heard her partner's breathless reply.

"Ooooookay," she groaned. "Don't wait up for me." The connection broken, Delia shook her head. She'd love to have sex but she wasn't going to pick up a man for a quick fix. She had her handy vibrator for that. Funny how some things had changed very little from Old Earth. *Guess it's hard to improve on a good thing and face it, the male anatomy hadn't changed in two thousand years so why should dildos.* Somehow the prospect of an evening, or even five minutes, with a substitute cock didn't really excite her. Visions of the bounty hunter from Tristar 234 appeared in her head and she felt herself grow wet and heavy between her legs in the Earth clothing. Her flight suit would have absorbed the moisture and kept her comfortable but the unfamiliar jeans just chafed her labia and heightened her need for a real cock, attached to a real man.

She was willing to bet that *he* would be able to satisfy a woman, all night long. His huge, powerful body had been like a well-honed machine. Light battle armor protected his torso but he wore none below the waist and she had to admit that she had checked out his package as he strode toward her. As he leaned into her, he had made sure she could feel his long, thick cock pressing against her as if it sought entry into her tight channel even then.

In some of the Old Earth romance novels that had survived, Delia had read that many Earth men were "hung like a stallion" and she had always wondered what that meant. Now she knew and all she wanted was for him to mount her from behind, thrust into her, biting her neck like the stallion covering his mare. He had known she could feel how aroused he was but instead of backing off or being embarrassed, he had pressed closer so that she would know how much of him she would have to accept when the time came. Her breasts had felt swollen and needy, her clit had poked out of its hood as if searching for him and the relief he would be able to give her. Even her flight uniform had felt as if it was too small for her body as his huge rod had pressed against her. She'd known he would have to prepare her well if she were to take his huge cock inside her.

Her head flooded with pictures of them in her cabin, the bounty hunter slowly undoing the zipper of her uniform, starting at the shoulder then going diagonally across her body, the first step in the journey to ready her body for him. The suit was formfitting and hugged her body, making it unnecessary to wear a bra. Would he be surprised when he lowered the zipper enough to reveal her generous breasts? Breasts that would be open to his gaze immediately. Would he be able to resist them or would he need to caress them with his mouth and tease them with his tongue, sucking them into his mouth, nipping their tips with his teeth? The old romance novels talked about that kind of loveplay but Delia had never experienced it. Nowadays everything was quick and efficient, done with a minimum of fuss, a minimum of effort and often with a minimum of pleasure.

Her bounty hunter bore the look of a man who wouldn't be easily bored. She could imagine him spending hours on her body, pleasuring her to the point of insanity. She knew her breasts were sensitive as she often brought herself release in her bed or in the shower and she loved how her nipples grew longer and harder with her own ministrations. She couldn't imagine the pleasure to be had at the hands and mouth of someone like him. Would he be a bit rough with her, pinching her nipples, making her cry in agony, the right kind of agony? Most men were intimidated by her since she was a decorated fighter but he'd been interested in the woman not the pilot. At least that was the message his rock-hard erection had passed to her and she'd been thrilled. Then he'd turned and walked away.

Forcing her way through the crowd, Delia headed for the exit portal leading to the station where her cruiser was docked. May as well get some sleep since she'd probably be at the helm alone tomorrow while Lina slept the morning away. She didn't begrudge her navigator her recreation time. Hell, she'd love to be doing the mattress mambo herself but she just couldn't work up interest in any other man. The bounty hunter probably didn't even remember her, let alone have any notion of finding her again. Better to go back to the ship and get some sleep.

Smacking her hand to her forehead, Delia remembered that she couldn't go back to the cruiser. She had to go back to the ranch. Yeehaw! She and Lina had a quaint little cabin all to themselves and they were not to return to their cruiser under any circumstances, Galactic Council's orders. The week was only just beginning and tomorrow was the trail ride followed by the evening barbecue. Her butt was probably going to be so sore she wouldn't be able to walk for a week, let alone close her legs, although that might not be such a bad thing given the right impetus to keep her legs open. Delia didn't want to know what kind of creature they were going to barbecue. She was almost positive that the pictures of the barbecue at the dude ranch that she had seen on her compugram showed a creature with six legs being roasted and she was sure that Earth cows didn't have six legs. Ergo an Earth cow was not being sacrificed for dinner. So what was? Perhaps she could just plead a headache and avoid the dilemma. The whole week seemed to stretch on in her mind, a string of activities she now realized she'd rather just avoid.

Steeling herself to the inevitable, she tried to make her way through the crowd to the brightly lit exit portal. The sea of bodies forced her to go slowly and she gritted her teeth against the number of hands reaching to squeeze her breast or run their hand down her butt cheek. It wasn't worth the time it took to push them away, easier to just get out of there onto one of the mobalks, as they called the mobile walkways that crisscrossed the city, that led to the ranch.

Turning her body to pass between two Arcadian knights, she felt not a hand but the featherlight touch on her neck again, like a lover's caress or the feel of silk on bare flesh. She knew that it would be futile to put up her hand as there would be nothing there but the feeling was disconcerting nonetheless. Her mother had always claimed that Delia had the "sight" and she certainly felt that someone was trying to read her without her knowledge yet she couldn't pick up who they were or even if they were in the room with her. She should have paid more attention when her mother encouraged her to work with a *malda* to develop her abilities but she was always too busy or too scared.

She breathed a sigh of relief as she wormed a path out of the crowd and made her way down the passageway to the exit portal. Delia didn't remember the corridor being so dark and that set off her internal radar but before she had a chance to set up a protective intrascreen, an arm snaked out and hauled her into the shadows.

"I told you I'd find you," a rough voice whispered as he claimed her with the tip of his tongue, just below her ear, just like last time.

Chapter Two

ꙮ

Jude had forgotten how luscious this woman was. He'd only had a chance to look before but this was a chance to touch, to claim. He could have used his scanner implants to scope out the room to find her but he didn't need them. Her scent was the only one in the room that he could pick up. It was as if the room was empty, save for her. Jude had to laugh that a woman who was such a hardened warrior could have such a delicate scent. He knew she would hate that.

Although the room was packed tightly with bodies, he could even detect the tangy, sea-smell between her legs. He wondered what she had been thinking about a few minutes ago when it had become almost overpowering to him. Had she been excited watching those pseudo-cowboys riding the mechanical bull? Had she been imagining one of them straddling her, pounding into her? God, he hoped not! He hoped she'd been thinking about him.

He wondered what she'd look like spread open for him. An old museum he had once visited displayed some relics from Old Earth and among them was a beautiful, big shell. It was a coral-pink color and looked as smooth as silk to the touch. Were her cunt lips that same delicate shade? Would they have secrets like those hidden inside the shell? At the museum he had wanted to reach through the protectascreen to stroke the smoothness of the conch shell and now he found himself wanting to do the same thing to her, strip her naked, lay her down on the table in his cabin and feast on those succulent lips until she came screaming against his mouth.

She stiffened in his arms and he knew she would go for the knife she kept hidden in her torso armor. He also knew she was going to be very angry when she realized she was wearing tight jeans and a t-shirt not her body-hugging armored suit. Her thoughts pounded into him, her emotions flooding along behind. He didn't need his scanner implants with this woman. He was so attuned to her that her thoughts melded with his. That was going to piss her off too!

As he held her against himself he thought about her reaction to his body scan. His implants were so sensitive, so high-tech that the lab jockeys had assured him that no one, absolutely no one would know they were being scanned but he'd seen her reaction. She knew she was being invaded and she knew he was there—two impossibilities according to the lab guys. How'd she do it?

Just as he predicted, as soon as he released her arm she went for her knife.

"Shit," she exploded through clenched teeth as she realized the knife wasn't there. Her shirt didn't allow for a hidden knife and he knew she didn't have one in her bra. Her pebbled nipples made it delightfully obvious that she wasn't wearing one. Pulling her arm down between them, he let her hand rest on his erection. That was just a safety technique to protect her. It had nothing to do with him wanting her hand on his cock or wanting her to feel how long and thick with want he was.

For once he was glad to be wearing Old Earth garb, popular on the cowboy planet. The worn jeans let her feel how her closeness affected him and he knew that if he turned her in his arms, her pert nipples would be pressed against the soft material of his t-shirt. His regular body armor would never allow him to feel the curves of her body or the quickness of her breath as he held her firmly against him, but the worn jeans let him pull her to him and mold her body to his.

Despite the fact that he would love to hold her in his arms forever, Jude had no more time to waste trying to persuade this ornery woman to join him. His navigator's life was at stake and the time for dancing around each other was past so he activated his implants again to hasten his persuasion.

I'm going to take you with me to The Renegade. *You are delighted to come with me and will cause no trouble.* Jude put his arm around Delia as if to shepherd her along to his ship when he flinched from her response that pounded loud and clear in his head.

I am not delighted to go with you and I can promise you that I will cause no end of trouble, so I suggest you back off now and let me go. A wry smile lit up Jude's face. He had no idea she was going to present such a challenge for him and if she had even a tiny suspicion of how much that pleased him, she'd have been happy to blast him into another dimension. Nobody had ever been able to resist the suggestions from his implants. Hell, that's what they were for, yet this woman threw them back in his face, with gusto. Maybe he needed to try a little honesty.

"You're a difficult woman to keep up with," he whispered in her ear. "Every planet I visited had your scent still in the air but you were gone."

"You could smell me after I was gone?" she asked incredulously.

"As soon as I stepped out of the ship, your tangy scent caught me but I could tell I had just missed you," he said, gently nudging her cheek, almost like a cat. He felt her make the mistake of relaxing her guard for a moment and leaning into his body. That was the opportunity Jude had been waiting for. Gently stroking the side of her face, he touched her with his sensor-bracelet and she collapsed in his arms.

Well, he had used a little honesty, coupled with a bit of treachery, but his navigator needed him and time was running out. It was easy to clear a path from the club, claiming his girlfriend had too much to drink. Standing off to one side in the landing bay, he held her gently against him while he called his ship to pick them up. A small speeder pod appeared almost immediately and two crew members scrambled out to assist him. Jude nearly threw them to the ground when they tried to help. Backing off quickly, they pulled out the floating transpod and watched as Jude gently laid her down. He allowed them to carefully realign the transpod inside its cradle in the little craft and set the holding beams but at his fierce scowl, they scrambled to return to the safety of the cockpit. Crawling in to secure himself to the bench beside her, he gave the order to return to *The Renegade.*

He knew the pod crew was trying to contain their curiosity but he also knew he had provoked their interest by refusing to let them help. His crew was used to dealing with a man who showed no softness, no mercy. He was fair but they knew he was a man you didn't cross. This considerate man was someone they didn't recognize and frankly, neither did he. He felt such a possessiveness for this woman that he didn't want her out of his sight or out of his arms. Knowing she wouldn't waken until they were on *The Renegade,* he felt safe taking her hand and gently stroking the back of it. Even though she was out, he wanted her to be comforted, to know she wasn't alone. She was going to be mad enough when she woke up that any damage control he could do in advance would be well worth it.

The little speeder pod shot through the night sky past the planet's two pink moons to rendezvous with the cruiser hidden behind the second moon. Jude watched *The Renegade*'s rear hatch open in a giant yawn and the pod sailed into the landing bay. As soon as the craft came to a halt, Jude deactivated the beams holding the transpod in its cradle and when the rear door opened, he guided the transpod as it floated free of the small vessel.

His crew held back, waiting for his signal to approach and when he gave a quick nod, two came forward to manipulate the pod through the rabbit warren of passageways inside the ship. When they went to take her to the infirmary, Jude growled that she was to go to his quarters. As the doors to his cabin slid shut, he had a last look at the two crew members who were staring unabashed, eager to apprise their shipmates of what they had seen. Jude found that he didn't care. This woman's comfort meant more to him than any crew gossip. Crossing to the bed, he carefully set her down, reluctant to let go. He wanted to undress her but that would have to wait until she came to. Making love to her was inevitable and he had waited this long to have her so another few minutes would make no difference. When he stripped her and worshipped her body, he wanted her to howl with delight. He wanted her wet with longing, ripe with desire. Oh yeah, he could wait!

Chapter Three

ꩡ

Delia struggled to the surface, her head woozy and heavy. Surely she hadn't had that much to drink. Slowly the haze dissipated enough to let her focus on what the hell had happened to her and where in Bartalian she was! Snippets of information scuttled through her mind—Lina waving as she went man-hunting, men flying off the mechanical bull, groping hands as she tried to wend her way through the crowd, a rock-hard body holding her close, the feel of that huge hard-on against her back, a hand stroking her face then nothing.

That bastard! Somehow he'd zapped her and knocked her out but where in Jobin's name was she now? Furtively, she opened her eyes enough to see her surroundings and realized she was in a cabin of an old Maladian cruiser. Her father had flown one of these for the Galactic Council, shepherding VIPs around the galaxy and she was well aware that these cruisers had been used strictly to transport small parties of government bigwigs and while they were reliable transport ships they had little speed and restricted maneuverability. She was certain her captor had made modifications to the cruiser. The plan was brilliant really. Take an old Maladian cruiser and give it massive firepower and state-of-the-art engines and you have a wolf in sheep's clothing. She smiled as she realized that she wouldn't have expected anything less from *him*.

A soft hiss signaled the opening of a door but Delia kept her eyes closed, desperate to keep any advantage. Slowly opening her eyes a slit, she bit back a gasp. The gasp was partly shock as she had a first look at her captor, the bounty hunter from Tristar 234 and partly from the fact that he had entered the cabin and, unaware that she was awake, had begun to strip.

Sitting down in a straight-back chair, he pulled off his boots and socks then, standing and keeping his back to her, he grabbed his t-shirt, pulled it over his head and threw it onto a floating armchair. This time Delia had to struggle to stifle a moan as the muscles in his sculpted back shifted with the movement. She watched, spellbound, as he raised his hands above his head and, linking his fingers, stretched. He was so beautiful. His muscles were well defined, not heavy and bulky and Delia realized that even the tufts of hair she could see under his arms seemed erotic. She had never wanted to run her fingers through a man's hair there before but she just knew it would be soft and silky, a contrast to the coarse wiry hair that would surround that thick, glorious penis.

He must have read her thoughts about his rod for Delia heard the sound of a zipper being lowered. She resisted the urge to open her eyes, any small advantage was an advantage. Through her lowered lashes, she watched as he stuck his thumbs in the waistband of his jeans and pulled them down over his slim hips and off. Commando in the twenty-fifth century! Gotta love a man who keeps with tradition! His ass was smooth and firm and she could see his cock hanging between his legs. By *Panton*! It was so long lying there at rest, what would it be like when he was aroused, ready to take her?

Wait a minute! Who said he was going to have her? When did that become the future not a question? Inevitability?

I know you're awake, his voice whispered to her. Her eyes flew open as he turned to face her, letting her have her first view of his impressive cock.

It seems to do that as soon as it knows you're near. She could hear the laughter even in his inner voice. Now his cock was long and thick with a beautiful bow in it as if it was too long and heavy to stand up straight and bent to kiss his navel instead. The element of surprise gone, if it was ever there, she raised her head on her bent arm and looked her fill. His chest was smooth, his abs as solid as rock but his cock dominated the picture in her mind. It was all she could do not to crawl across the bed, crawl across the floor and crawl up his body to take that massive cock into her mouth, into her body. She didn't think she was going to be able to take him without pain.

Don't you know that's what it's all about? The pleasure with the pain.

Are you focusing all my attention on your cock?

Maybe.

As Delia stared, she could see his cock grow longer and thicker. That bow in it would let it touch places inside her no man had ever touched, send her spinning off in a million directions. Eyes flying up to his face, Delia saw him smile at her. It was a tender smile but the wolf was still there waiting to get out.

You're the one making me hard as classen. *Your thoughts mirror mine but they're your thoughts.*

Delia knew it was true. She didn't need his thoughts to know how much she wanted him, had wanted him since the first time she saw him.

"Why have you followed me?" she asked, rising to stand in front of him.

"I think you already know the answer to that. I have to have you," he said gruffly. He hoped she wasn't able to read the struggle in his head. He had to have her to save his navigator but now it was much more than that. He had to have *her*. He needed her like he needed to fly, to fight, to breathe and he wasn't sure he liked that. Toryn was what this was all about. Wasn't it? He had to rescue Toryn and this woman was the key. She was Brachan's weakness. Jude knew Brachan would do anything to have her, even release Toryn.

Delia wanted to know more. She knew he was desperately hiding something and she could feel the shield he had erected in his mind keeping her out. He felt anguish for someone named Toryn and somehow she was part of a plan but before she could ask he gently took her head in his hands and put his lips to hers. It was a gentle kiss, more an apology than a kiss, then he unleashed the full force of his passion for her. Sliding his fingers through her hair, he trapped her while his tongue traced the sensitive underside of her top lip. She shivered.

You like that?

You know I do.

Taking advantage of her acquiescence, Jude took little nips all along her top lip. He had never had a chance to study her beautiful face before, to notice that her bottom lip was a bit larger than her top lip, giving her a pouty just-out-of-bed look. He thrust his tongue into her mouth and was delighted to feel her touch at it, tentatively at first then trying to eat at him as if she wanted to swallow him whole. He sensed that she was inexperienced, maybe her previous lovers had been too quick, too eager. He intended to rectify that, to take his time, to make her howl.

Delia was way out of her league. She could fly a cruiser through a battlesky or land on the head of a pin but her sexual encounters had been infrequent and unsatisfying. *That's all about to change.* Delia laughed, glad he had read her mind so he would know to take it easy with her, to be gentle. *I said it was about to change. No way am I going to take it easy or be gentle. I'm going to fuck you 'til you howl.*

He grabbed her t-shirt and pulled it up over her head. His cock was so long and hard that she could feel it crawling up the bare skin of her belly like a living thing. Delia put her hands on his shoulders as he sank to his knees in front of her.

"Lift your foot!" he ordered. Delia obediently lifted her foot to let him pull off her sock and boot. When had she become such an obedient slave? Perhaps when she saw what was hanging between his legs and was going to be pushing its way inside her.

"Now the other one!" he commanded. Sneaking a look at his cock as she lifted her foot, she saw the prominent veins in his erection pounding in tandem with his heart, the first drops of pre-cum slipping out. How she wanted to reach down and slide the very tip of her tongue into that little slit, to have that first taste of him, of his precious fluid. How was that going to feel as he pushed through her tiny opening into her tight little channel? She knew she hadn't had enough partners to make his entry easy. The thought of that huge cock pushing past her opening, forcing her channel to give way and let him in was enough to send a jolt of cream rushing out of her cunt.

As Jude grabbed hold of her panties and jeans and tugged them down her legs, he was blindsided by her thoughts of him pushing his way inside her. He could feel how hard she was going to squeeze him as he made her body yield, inch by inch, as he breached her passage. He could feel her turning liquid for him and, yanking her jeans and panties off, quickly spread her legs to lap at her cunt as her tangy cream seeped out.

Delia wasn't sure whether to be mortified or delighted but the decision was quickly made for her as she felt his talented tongue tucking its way into her entry and eating her whole. He took his time, waiting until every drop of nectar had slipped into his mouth then licked along her delicate folds to retrieve any honey hidden there. He flexed his tongue up under her little hood, tickling her clit, bringing it to life. Delia had no idea that people made love like this, could make love like this. Her few forays into the sexual arena hadn't involved much enjoyment of her body, for her or for her partner. She couldn't wait to get her chance to explore his magnificent body. She wondered if he'd like her to take him into her mouth the way he'd done to her. Would he like that or would he find it unpleasant? Guess she'd just have to find out for herself and there was no time like the present.

Placing her hands on his shoulders, she shoved him away and stepped back. Jude sat back on his haunches, perplexed as to why she wanted him to stop. Delia's face took on a naughty smile and putting her hands on her hips, she ordered him to stand up. A wicked grin broke out on Jude's face as she wrested control from him. Nothing like a gorgeous, naked woman ordering you to do her bidding to give you a major cockstand. This could prove to be very interesting, for him and for her. He sensed her inexperience but also sensed her curiosity and sense of adventure. He knew that as a pilot she took risks and always pushed herself to the limit so he was delighted to fantasize that she would approach making love in the same way.

Once on Antelika, Delia had a chance to view some artifacts from Old Earth and had been captivated by a statue of a naked man. She remembered what a surprise it had been for her to see the beauty of the male form. That statue had crowded her thoughts and dreams for weeks but it was just a pale shadow compared to the impact of this man's nude form. Wearing his body armor and weapons, he was a formidable sight yet unclothed he dominated her senses. It was as if the coverings were just that, coverings, totally unnecessary on his splendid frame. His dark, silky hair brushed his shoulders drawing her eyes to their width. It was all she could do not to run her hands through the silken mass, across his shoulders and down his massive arms. That beautiful hair should have looked out of place on his warrior body but, if anything, it only enhanced his masculine beauty. Even his legs were the legs of a medieval knight, hard and muscular as if he spent hours in the saddle.

He stood, unmoving, as she completed her leisurely perusal of his imposing frame. She could tell by the way he was flexing his hands at his sides that he wasn't as calm and collected as he seemed. As she went to her knees in front of him, she looked up to see him throw back his head, clenching his fists in anticipation. He hissed as she put out one finger and wiped away the little tear of pre-cum. "Watch me," she ordered as she opened her mouth and set her finger on her tongue. It appeared that he couldn't look away as she closed her mouth and slowly pulled out her finger. "Mmmm. You taste delicious," she whispered. He groaned. That was the answer she needed. He loved it as much as she did.

As he watched, spellbound, Delia licked up the length of her forefinger then ran her moist finger down his cock, starting at the little slit, over the thick head then down the entire length. As soon as her finger finished its journey, she leaned forward to allow her tongue to follow the same path back up. Even though he knew what she was going to do, Jude couldn't stop his body from tensing in anticipation, from almost flinching as her pink tongue peeked out from between her lips. To torment him, she used only the very point, making it rigid and tracing up his stiff cock over the heavy collar to the tip. Taking him in both hands, Delia placed a kiss on the head then sent his senses spinning by placing her mouth over him. He looked on, not daring to breathe, as he felt her forcing her body to relax and take him deeper into her mouth. She was inexperienced but the bombardment of senses flashing into his head told of curiosity, delight and a desire to please him. She needn't have worried about that. The instant his cock had entered the warm cavern of her mouth, the galaxy could have melted around them and he wouldn't have noticed.

He felt as if he were going into sensory overload with the mélange of feelings from him and from her. He could taste himself, taste the pleasure she was feeling. He felt his cock in her mouth but through her also felt the sensation of having it in his own mouth, feeling the heavy veins, the huge head gagging him, the smooth skin over the rock-hard shaft. He knew he should feel repulsed by it all but he wasn't. It felt familiar, delicious. His head was reeling with his own lust as she sucked in her cheeks and clutched him tightly yet it was compounded with the lust from her body that careened around his head as well. It was almost like he had two cocks each being pleasured simultaneously, one by him and one by her. He could smell her arousal, smell her cream, feel her clit swelling, her tissues ripening. His own orgasm was welling up inside but coupled with the imminence of her own, he felt like his skin was too tight, his body too electrified.

Delia couldn't believe what was happening. She sensed his surprise as their feelings blended and he felt what she felt. Now he knew the sensation of having that enormous hard-on down his throat, of running his tongue over the smooth skin, the veins bulging and pulsing. She felt his surprise turn to curiosity then to desire as he learned the texture of his own skin, the taste of himself. Then she began to feel the changes in her body through his heightened senses. Her cream smelled delicious, like a succulent dessert, and her clit swelled, eager for the friction his erection would bring. She knew he could feel her channel softening, waiting for him to push his way in. Suddenly he put his hands to her head and broke the connection. Before she had time to protest, he pulled her to her feet and caught her in his arms.

"No way am I going to come in your mouth the first time we make love," he growled. "I want to be deep inside you when I come. I want you to howl and bite when you come." He strode across the cabin, his cock pulsing, trapped between their bodies as he walked. Laying Delia gently on the bed, he rolled her to her stomach and, pulling her onto her hands and knees, crouched on the floor at the end of the bed. As he spread her legs, he was rewarded with a lovely view of her shimmery slit. It was as beautiful as he'd expected, just like the conch shell from the museum. The skin was pink and luscious and oh-so wet. Leaning forward, he licked a path from her clit back to her entrance, delighted as she shivered. Running the outsides of his hands up her inner thighs, he got to his feet, grabbing hold of his hard-on with one hand to position it. He slid home to the hilt, remaining motionless as he gently caressed her back. He could feel her fluttering around his shaft, gently massaging it with her internal muscles then, with a subtle shift, her feelings began to run alongside his own in his head. He gradually became aware that what he was now feeling was what she felt when he was inside her. It was no longer just the pulsing of his cock. Instead he had become part of her with Delia tightening her channel around him. Through her body, he felt her tighten herself and grab hold of him yet he also felt his cock being squeezed. The double sensation was driving him crazy. Was he feeling through himself or was he feeling through her? Now he felt his own cock pulsing, growing, hardening as it lay inside them. He loved to stroke in and out of a woman but what would it be like to be part of her while she had his long, strong phallus pumping her like a piston. He would be making love as a man but feeling it as a man and a woman.

His hands were gently caressing her back but now it was as if someone was stroking him as well and he shivered to realize that what he felt was himself stroking his back. Each time his hands moved up and down her back, he felt the companion strokes along his. He ran his fingertips along her shoulders and back across her shoulder blades, the response making his body quiver. Using his forefinger, he traced down her spine, lingering on each delicate indentation and was delighted to feel a finger tracing the same path along his backbone.

He could look down and see his granite erection, held securely inside her but what he was feeling was that rock-hard penis inside himself and he loved it. As he watched, he began to rock in and out of her, in and out of him and the roof started to lift off. It was as if he had this beautiful open vagina and his whole being was centered on the powerful strokes of his own massive erection inside it. Gently swaying forward and back, his cock massaged inside them. He loved making love, loved having a big, powerful penis to pleasure her but being able to be part of what she was feeling as that ramrod stroked in and out of her was indescribable. Reaching between her legs, he nudged her clit with his finger and felt the odd sensation of touching a corresponding clit sitting just above his penis. He could feel the physical sensation of his penis sliding in and out coupled with the mental sensation of her stimulated clit. He didn't know whether to focus on his staff as it pleasured her or to focus on the hard little pseudo-clit perched just above it. Every stroke of his cock made that little nub hum and made her howl.

Delia didn't have much experience with lovers but she'd made love enough times to know this was way beyond the bounds of ordinary. What in Bartalian was happening to her? She was so embarrassed when he put her on hands and knees and then just looked at her. She wanted to close her legs but she also wanted to open them wider and invite him in. When he licked her juicy cunt she couldn't believe people made love like that. She wanted to push him away and she wanted him to never, ever stop. But as soon as he began to push that enormous cock inside her, her head began to spin and suddenly she knew exactly what he was feeling as it pushed past her tiny opening and into her vagina. She felt his penis being gripped by those muscles so she tightened them and shared his delight as his cock was seized tight. Then he began to move, rubbing the walls of her channel as he slid in and out, nudging her clit.

She'd always wondered why men made such a big deal about their penis. Now she knew! It was a weapon of incredible pleasure which he wielded like a champion and she got to share it with him. She could feel her body receiving his massive cock as it hammered into her but she also felt his cock and his intense pleasure as his body slapped against hers, pleasure that was too much to bear. She might have been able to hang on if the pleasure had been only hers but it was just too strong coupled with his and she felt them tumbling to the edge then over. She felt him throw his arms to each side of her to give his last few thrusts more power. She felt him catch the skin of her back with his teeth and bite her. She howled as she felt the rush of cum jetting from his cock, flooding her with his strength.

He might have been able to hold on longer but not when their emotions were so tightly linked. He could feel her orgasm gathering so he put his hands on each side of her on the bed and slammed into her with his battering ram. He couldn't be gentle, knowing each thrust would rub their clit. Leaning over her back, he put his teeth to her and bit her, bit him! Hallelujah! She howled! The double stimulation was more than any genetically engineered transplants could handle and as his cum shot into her, he was ecstatic that she was able to push past all his barriers and meld with him. He felt his rich, thick seed leave his body then became one with her as her passage received his precious fluid. He felt her womb throbbing as it took his essence deep inside. Thank Jobin his implants made pregnancy impossible for he knew he was potent with this woman! A baby wasn't in his future. He was happy doing what he did. He wasn't ready to settle down. At least not until he found a woman who could stand up to him, a strong woman, a powerful woman. A woman like this one?

All Delia could do was utter a prayer of thanks to the doctors who looked after the pilots who flew for the Wardelian League. They made sure her subcutaneous implants were up-to-date and active and this was one time she was sure she needed to be protected against pregnancy. As his seed rushed into her, she could feel how thick and potent it was. Perhaps it was because her body was the receptacle for the rich cream or because she shared his thoughts as it screamed into her but no matter what the reason she knew they were playing with fire. Thank goodness she didn't need to worry about having his child! It was a good thing, wasn't it?

Then why did she see him cradling a tiny baby in his big hands, looking adoringly down at the precious bundle? Why did she see him watching her as she nursed, running his hand gently over the downy hair on the baby's head? Why did she see a little child running to be scooped up by a handsome man who looked suspiciously like her bounty hunter? She came to the realization that she had made mad, passionate love with this man, like she had done with no other and she didn't even know his name. Even now, that seemed unimportant. A name wouldn't change the connection they had, make it any more secure. That would be impossible. She was in big trouble with a capital T.

Pulling gently out of her, Jude felt the link weaken then disappear completely and he felt oddly bereft. Unwilling to dwell on what had just happened, he rolled to his side, pulling her down with him. He felt her body relax as she moved into the curve of his body then sleep claimed him.

Delia lay quietly tucked in the cocoon of his body, listening to his gentle breathing, wondering how she had gotten into this situation. It was supposed to be an impromptu holiday with her navigator and now it had turned into…what? Her connection to this man was more than that, it was more like a bonding. Would he let her go? Would he let her get back to her job? Did she want him to let her go? As these tumultuous thoughts tumbled around in her head, sleep finally came.

Chapter Four

ꟹ

This time when Delia woke, she knew exactly where she was and who brought her there. His warm scent was in the air all around her and the smell of their lovemaking clung to her skin. She was pinned to the solid body behind her by a steely arm, her own arm small and pale as it lay on top. His fingers were long and calloused—hard to imagine how delicate they had been with her. Small scars decorated the back of his hand, indicative of the life he led. She knew this man was dangerous and deadly but she was drawn to him, belonged to him and he to her. She knew the instant he awakened, his steely rod pulsing between her cheeks. Her body wept with delight at the feel of his massive weapon, poised for entry. How long was he going to make her wait? She felt the subtle shift of his body to move his erection to her entrance then he gently slid inside. She knew they needed no protection for their respective implants protected not only against pregnancy but against disease as well.

Jude was delighted to awaken to feel her spooned against him, his arm holding her to him, where she belonged. His sexual encounters were usually through need not desire so more often than not he woke up alone. He knew this woman was his fate but he couldn't let that interfere with his rescue of Toryn. He felt the moment she reconnected with him, sensing her wetness, her need for him to fill her. Her body was warm and pliant, her opening wet and juicy as he slid in from behind and held there, savoring the connection. He could have spent eternity like that with her tight inner muscles clutching him but he felt her move up then slide back down his solid erection and he knew he would never be able to remain motionless.

Putting both arms around her, he rolled to his back, stretching his legs with her atop him.

Delia understood immediately and sat up, keeping his penis tightly clenched inside her. By bending her legs and leaning forward, she was able to grip his rock-hard thighs, giving her the leverage she needed to lift herself up and almost off his erection then back down, slowly, ever-so slowly, inch by inch.

Then she felt the shift as he began to invade her head to bond with her but this time she threw up a screen to keep him out. She was delighted to feel him reel back mentally and smile at her boldness. Maybe she had learned more from her grandmother about this gift than she realized. It was much too soon for her body and mind to undergo the same connection they had had the last time. It had been excruciatingly wonderful but all-consuming as well. This time she wanted to go slowly to let her body savor the lovemaking without the power of his feelings too.

Jude knew what she was about and he was surprised to find that he agreed with her. It had been almost too intense when they were making love and he didn't know how often he wanted to tempt Fate in that way. This was just temporary until he rescued Toryn. No sense letting feelings get in the way. Just enjoy it while it lasts then move on. He felt her voice.

Are you angry that I blocked you?

I was surprised but in some ways grateful.

What do you mean?

I automatically try to link with you. I can't stop it but everything was so intense last time that it would be nice to take it slow and easy this time.

I love what we did together earlier but now I want to savor you.

Sounds good to me!

Jude ran his hands up the curve of her back as she leaned away from him. Of course that wasn't disappointment he felt when there was no answering tingle along his back. Then she began to ride him and all he could think about were the feelings concentrated in his cock. She was wet and tight and clenched him like a fist. Each time she lifted up he was able to see his phallus, shiny with her juice, as it emerged from her entrance then she would sink down and he would see it disappear inside her to be grabbed by the strong muscles in her canal. He couldn't understand how she could fit that massive erection inside her. Even though they weren't connected mentally, the sight of that solid hard-on entering her made his own tiny hole pucker in anticipation. He wanted to squirm as he envisioned a great, big cock entering him, separating the tender flesh as it forced its way inside. He needed to rescue Toryn!

Delia reveled in the sensation of being filled by his enormous cock. She couldn't fathom how she was able to swallow all of it but each stroke took him so far inside her that her entire body quivered. With her back to his front the angle of penetration was unusual for her, especially as she was astride him and each stroke rubbed her clit with that great bowed cock. Toooo much! With one last downstroke, she felt her body tighten until her skin felt too small then the ripples of pleasure began to flow from her tiny clit to invade her entire body. She heard him groan, felt him shove inside her as far as he could then let go, filling her with rivers of cum. Even without their connection, she could feel the force of his orgasm as it entwined with hers. She hung there, limp, until he took her by the shoulders and pulled her back to lie on his chest. His shaft slowly slid from her body to lie against her thigh. She had to laugh as even his penis seemed exhausted.

Delia lay quiescent as he put his hand between her legs, dipping his finger in the copious liquid. She shivered as he ran his finger along her labia, stopping to dip into her tight little entry hole. His long finger explored the delicate inner tissue, still sensitive and swollen from her orgasm. Using it like a miniature penis, he swung it in and out of her then used her lubricant as he teased her clitoris. He rubbed her clit in gentle circles then flicked its sensitive hood, making her cry out.

"Did I hurt you?" he asked, concerned.

"No. It doesn't hurt but I'm so sensitive there that I can hardly stand for you to touch me."

"I can make it all better," he said slyly. "Would you like me to do that for you?" Trembling, she nodded acquiescence. Sliding out from underneath her, he pushed himself off the foot of the bed and went to his knees between her legs. "Scoot your butt to the bottom of the bed so I can start to make it better," he said.

Bending her legs, Delia slid her rear down the bed until it was right at the edge. With gentleness, he pressed her legs apart then placed them over his shoulders. Using his thumbs, he opened her folds to reveal her succulent portal, drenched in his cream. Leaning forward, he set his tongue to her and licked a path up her crease. She tried to squirm away but he put his hands on her butt cheeks to keep her in position. "Ah, ah, ah," he said. "I can't make it all better if you don't stay still for me." Then he poked his strong tongue right into her entry, licking her juicy hole with it. How did he expect her to keep still while he tortured her like that? Withdrawing his tongue, he licked her generous folds up to her nub which stood upright to welcome him. Tucking his tongue under the little hood, he tickled at her with the very tip, the point zeroing right in on her pleasure spot. "Does that feel better yet?" he asked, drawing his mouth back. Delia's answer was a moan. "I guess I'd better keep trying."

Putting his hands under her legs, he forced her butt up in the air to expose her tiny puckered hole. Sensing his intent, Delia tried to close her legs to him but he was too strong. Coating his finger first with their cream, he delicately touched the circle that was drawn so tight. He didn't try to push his way in. Instead he was content to trace the ridges that surrounded her little rosette. As soon as he felt her relax, he carefully pushed inside, giving her time to adjust to the unfamiliar invasion. Letting her become accustomed to the feeling, Jude worked his finger gently in and out then leaned forward to lick her slit at the same time.

Instead of the distaste she thought she would feel, Delia felt herself reaching for an orgasm. It's just too much, Delia thought. She could feel his finger inside her while he licked her slit then he withdrew it and pushed her butt higher in the air. She closed her eyes tightly as he put his tongue where no one but him had touched before. She screwed her eyes shut as he penetrated her ever-so slightly then they flew open as he let her bottom back down on the bed, keeping her legs on his shoulders. She opened her eyes to see him grab hold of his cock and slide it into her vagina.

All the sensations were so close to the surface that she screamed and orgasmed immediately he entered her. He continued pounding into her, he letting his own sensations build and build until at last he flew off, jetting into her. Delia felt the hot rush of semen as it flooded her. She watched as he threw back his head and closed his eyes, his jaw rigid from the exquisite pleasure, his torso covered in a faint sheen of sweat.

Jude stood for a moment, waiting for his heartbeat to return to normal as he tried to gather his thoughts and feelings about this woman. Even with her shield in place, making love with this woman was scary. He could feel her absolute trust in him, letting him enjoy her body, knowing that it would bring pleasure for them both. No one but Toryn had that trust in him and he wasn't sure how to deal with it. Maybe he needed to stick to the plan and start thinking about Toryn. His navigator would be counting on him, trusting him and he couldn't let him down. Stepping back, he gently placed her legs on the bed and let his cock slide free of her tight embrace.

Delia watched him step back but knew that more than his body had moved away, he had somehow detached himself from her. He quickly erected a sensorscreen to keep her from poking around in his mind but she knew there was something else going on here that he didn't want her to find out about.

She just didn't know what it was. Her grandmother would just tell her to wait and see what the Fates had in store for her.

She watched as he went into an adjoining room and heard him running water. Getting to her feet, she followed him and found herself in a luxurious bathroom with a commode and some sort of intricate shower chamber with multiple showerheads and seats. She couldn't stop herself from going over to look but she was unable to determine how all those heads would be used. Why would you want or need seats in a shower? She was at a loss to figure it out.

"I can leave if you would like to use the facilities," Jude said quietly. Delia turned slowly around, aware that he could read her silent questions and also aware that he wasn't going to furnish any answers.

Instead of responding, she walked over to him and said, "Do you realize that I've had your cock in my mouth and deep inside me? I've trusted you with my body with a trust no other man has shared. I've let down all my barriers with you, yet I don't even know your name." Whatever she was going to say, Jude hadn't expected that.

"I'm Jude Roland," he said.

"And I'm—"

"Delia Monroe," he said before she could finish. "Do you really think I would follow a woman halfway across the galaxy without knowing her name?"

Delia knew something wasn't right about this whole situation but before she could ask, Jude turned to leave, saying, "I'll just give you some privacy for a few minutes, if you like?"

She knew he was hiding something from her but every time she probed his thoughts, he shut her out immediately. She was afraid that she wasn't going to like his secret but until he was willing to share it with her, there wasn't much she could do. Making use of the commode and washing her hands, she went to stand at the shower stall again. Putting her hands to the wall of glass, she shuddered as visions began to flow into her head of Jude, standing naked, the warm water sluicing down his powerful body. She could see two hands on his chest, lathering his muscular torso with soap as the water poured over them. The hands gently washed him then slid down his body to encompass his erection—an erection that was hard and throbbing for release. She watched as Jude threw back in head in rapture, the muscles in his neck taut with ecstasy and his approaching orgasm. She felt like a voyeur as the shadowy figure ran a hand up and down Jude's rampant phallus, increasing the pressure little by little. She looked on as Jude put his hand atop the other and together they took up the hypnotic rhythm, up, down, up, down until, with a hoarse cry, he came over their joined hands. Delia didn't know if this was the past or the future, his past or her future. She didn't even know if she was the shadowy figure with him.

"Would you like to try out the shower?" he said in her ear. Delia nearly jumped out of her skin. How had he managed to sneak up on her like that? Usually this man put all her senses on high alert but she had retreated so far into her vision that he was able to blindside her. "Are you all right?" he asked, concern in his voice when he saw her face. He thought she had been planning to make use of the shower but that was not what he was sensing from her. What had she seen with her hands pressed to the glass? Did she know? Could she see?

Delia knew not to ask about her vision. If they got into the shower together, maybe it would happen. If it was her future. Taking his hand, she stepped into the beautiful glassed-in enclosure, pulling him in with her. Maybe this way she would find out some of his secrets. She sensed him erecting his screens to keep her out but that was fine. Let them do this with no extras, just the visceral attitudes.

Jude knew she was looking for answers but he was not ready to give them, plus he wasn't the only one involved. Other players were waiting in the wings.

"Warm water, Number One," he called and the tallest showerhead turned on, sending a gentle spray over them. "Soap," he said, reaching his hand into a slot in the wall and a generous dollop of soap was dispensed. Rubbing his hands together first to work the soap into a lather, he gently massaged her breasts using the slippery soap to tantalize her as he pinched and pulled her nipples. She moved into his hands, trying to get as close to him as she could. He had the very talented hands typical of a fighter pilot and bounty hunter. He turned one hand fingers down and began a leisurely journey down her belly and over her mound to arrive at her slick opening. It was the perfect angle to touch her deep inside and she writhed, enraptured by his intimate caress. He could sense her delight as his finger moved to nudge her clit. He circled it slowly and easily, spreading it out and touching right in the center where he knew she was the most sensitive. The outcome was inevitable. Within minutes he had pushed her over the precipice and she was in free fall for him, spinning out of control, beyond the bounds of pleasure.

He could still feel the waves undulating through her as he picked her up and set her up on one of the seats in the showering chamber. The seat was cut deep and high into the wall to allow one to sit well back. It also had two small vertical bars on each side to let you pull yourself up onto the seat from the floor. Delia was going to finally get to experience one of the seats in the chamber.

"Lean back and spread your legs for me," Jude commanded. Delia realized that when she opened her legs for him the height of the shelf would put her right at eye level. She could tell by the feral look in his eyes that he was well aware of that fact. If she could take on Sarwinian invaders with nothing but her wits and her Pyrian cruiser then she could certainly face this bounty hunter. She opened her legs and he smiled.

"You are gorgeous here," Jude said as he traced a finger down her slit. "I love all the beautiful colors and textures. I remember a double sunset I once saw on Halnavina. The sky was filled with the same exquisite colors as the two suns set and I didn't think I would ever see the like again but you are just as gorgeous." Running his fingers down her pouty lips, he took hold of one and tugged. She was so ready for him that he could hardly hold on to her slick lips. "You look good enough to eat and I think I'll do just that," he whispered. He knew she wished he'd drop his sensorscreen so they could share this but he held it firmly in place. Thrusting out his tongue, he used it to follow the path of her crease up from her entrance to her taut little bud. Hooking it under the hood of her clit, he pressed up with the very point of his tongue.

Oh Jude. That feels so good. Delia was delighted as he opened the door to his mind just a bit.

You are delectable. So sweet. I could feast on you for eternity.

Delia wondered if this was a prelude to the scene from her vision. Was she the one rubbing her slick hands over his body? Was she the one grasping that massive erection? Was it her hand he covered as he stroked himself to fulfillment? Was it her hands that received his warm, slippery cum as he yelled his completion? She felt him nudge the door in his mind to keep her from coming too far inside. As he laved her cunt she found that she was past caring, especially when he sent her reeling to another orgasm.

"Number One, water off," he said and the water immediately shut off. "Number three, open," he called. Delia watched open-mouthed as a small door beside her slid up to reveal a hidden recess. "My navigator loves to tinker with stuff so when we refitted the cruiser, I let him go nuts in here," Jude said as he gestured around the shower chamber. "There are all kinds of crazy gadgets hidden in these walls." Jude reached inside and pulled out some things that Delia didn't recognize. She looked on curiously as he set them on one of the lower-level seats then turned back to her.

"Do you trust me, Delia?" he asked, uncertainty in his eyes. She knew that he was hiding something from her but she also knew he wouldn't hurt her so she nodded hesitantly. Now that he had her acquiescence, Jude reached down and picked up one of the objects and held it out on the flat of his hand so she could see it. Delia drew her eyebrows together as she looked at the unfamiliar object. It resembled the tail of a *rintel* like the one her sister Molly kept for a pet but instead of being black, this one was a gorgeous shade of honey brown. It was set into some type of holder so the short tail fanned out. Reaching into the soap slot, this time he called out "cream" not "soap" so when he withdrew his hand there was a dollop of turquoise cream in his palm.

Standing in front of her, he whispered to her, "Put your legs on my shoulders, Delia." She complied, unsure what he was about. Holding the tail in one hand, he put his other hand out flat and dabbed the tail into the cream, covering it in a rich lather. "Open your legs for me," he urged. She couldn't stop herself from doing as he asked. As she looked down, he began to use the object to spread the lather over her pubic hair. She broke into a smile as she realized it was nothing but a brush he was using to coat her with delightful foam. She smiled as he looked up at her then laughed when the brush tickled as he coated her labia in the creamy froth.

Jude knew she still didn't realize what he was doing but hoped she would be so far gone that she wouldn't be able to cry halt. That wasn't to be!

Delia watched as he reached to the low seat and picked up another article. She tried to draw back as she recognized it from a book she had read detailing life on Old Earth. Now she knew what was happening! It was a razor and she was covered in cream so he could shave her pubis!

"Jude. What are you doing?" she cried anxiously.

"I read somewhere that this would enhance a woman's pleasure and I wanted to do it for you." He felt like such a bastard lying to her but he had no choice. It was time to stick to the plan and even though she didn't know it yet she was an integral part of that plan. "I'll stop if you want me to," he lied, "but I think you'll like how it feels when we make love afterwards."

Delia decided that this whole trip was made up of firsts for her so she would try to relax and let him pleasure her. Jude made sure she was covered in shaving cream then began to draw the razor through the hair low on her belly. Delia tried not to move but it was a foreign feeling and disconcerting to have someone running a sharp implement across her skin.

"Number Four, gentle flow," he called and the head nearest them came on with a small stream of water so he could keep the razor clean. Delia wanted to close her eyes so she didn't have to watch herself being shaved by someone else but the whole picture was so erotic that it was impossible to shut them. It was so arousing to feel his fingers nudge then hold her labia to one side but to watch at the same time was delicious. He was very gentle and thorough. He touched her delicate tissue as if it were precious to him, carefully moving the razor alongside her labia then right down them, removing every vestige of hair until she was shiny and completely open to him.

"Number Four, off," he called. Picking up a hand sprayer, he called, "Number Six, gently on," and carefully washed away all traces until she was clean and totally hairless. "Number Six, off," he called as he set the hand sprayer back in its holder. Reaching up to his shoulders, he put his hands under Delia's legs and set her feet down on the small shelves protruding below the seat. The footholds were shaped to comfortably hold one's heels and the placement of them kept her legs spread wide. She began to understand a lot more about the workings of the shower chamber.

As soon as Jude placed her feet in the footholds, he stepped back to look at her naked glory. He was speechless as he looked at the most secret part of her, totally exposed to his hungry gaze. He had thought this part of her was beautiful and luscious before but nothing prepared him for the sight of her with nothing to hide her glorious folds and secret places. It was a feast for the senses and for a few minutes he let down his screens so she could share his hunger.

Delia's thoughts were bombarded with his visions of her naked cunt. She thought he would be repelled by the sight of her hairless pussy but the opposite seemed to be true. His hunger was all-consuming as he stared at her.

I need to have you right now. So saying, he bent forward and licked her exposed vulva, made ultra-sensitive by the so-recent shave. Delia's knuckles were white as she gripped the bars of the shower seat, just waiting for that first touch of his tongue to her heated flesh. Then she felt just the tip begin to touch her with a featherlight caress. He traced right up her plump lips, barely grazing them in his erotic journey then he pressed harder and pushed her labia flat as his tongue swept over them. With her shaved pussy there was absolutely nothing between her skin and his tongue and she was aching for him, for his touch. Finding her succulent center, he licked her, like a tiger to cream and it was sublime torture. It was more than she could bear but still not enough. She needed him closer then he opened his mind to her and she knew the bliss he was reaping as well.

Jude knew it was a bad idea to let down his screens but he wanted to share this with her. She had let him touch her in a most intimate way and he wanted to bond with her even if just for a few minutes. The first touch of his tongue made him think of the richest, most succulent delicacies of the galaxy. Sweet fruits from Galandria, exotic pastries from Numan, irresistible tree berries from Zaminder, all of them paled in comparison to the sweetness of her taste. Her lips were fleshy and ripe beneath his tongue but her center, her lush center was paradise in his mouth.

Through his memories all the delights he had savored tantalized her, but the sweetest of them all was the taste of her, rich and spicy, dark and musky. She was his tongue as he licked her fleshy lips, explored her luscious slit, penetrated her delectable entrance. Then she knew he knew that it wasn't enough.

Jude reached up, grabbed her by the waist and set her down on the floor of the shower chamber. Delia watched, voracious for him, as he backed up and sat down on a lower-level seat on the opposite side of the chamber. This time it was Jude who grabbed the vertical rails.

"Come here and mount me!" he said in a low voice. Suddenly the vision reappeared. She saw him sitting on that same seat with someone else preparing to mount him. She knew it wasn't her. Who was it? Before the picture became clear, she felt him shift his shield into place and the image was lost. He still didn't trust her with his secret.

Jude knew she had been so close that time. He couldn't risk letting her past his shields again. She was too strong and he was proving to be too weak where she was concerned. "Come to me," he said. "Take me inside you." Delia walked forward, her smooth, swollen lips feeling foreign between her legs. Taking hold of the rails, she noticed there were footholds below this seat as well so she was able to put her feet in them and slide down his huge, glorious cock. She was unprepared for the added sensation of her bare cunt. There was no hair to come between her and his glorious body. His crisp hairs rubbed deliciously against her nether lips, adding to the delightful friction. Every downstroke brought them together while every upstroke made her draw in her breath in anticipation. Holding on to the bars and keeping her feet in the footholds allowed her to rise up until he was barely inside her then she could slam down on him, taking him as far inside her as she could. Sitting on his lap, face-to-face, so close to him, she was able to watch his face as the change came over him and she knew he was close. She felt his body tighten then he filled her with his juice, filled her until it ran from her in rivulets, down her thighs and over his. She slumped forward and Jude cradled her in his arms, rubbing gentle circles on her back.

Using her hands on the bars, Delia finally lifted herself off him and stood. She wished he would let her in. She missed the closeness of being linked to him but it was not to be. At least not for now. "Will the gadgets work for me?" she asked.

"Oh, most definitely," he said with a smile. "Go ahead and try them out."

Taking the hand sprayer, she called, "Number Six, gently on," and was delighted when the water began to flow in a gentle stream. Putting her hand in the slot she called for soap and a small quantity was dispensed in her palm. Jude's muscles tightened as he waited for her to wash him clean but after rubbing her hands together, she began to soap her breasts, forcing him to watch. She rubbed the soap all over her belly and under her arms. He swallowed as she put her hand in the slot and called for more soap. This time she lathered her hands and while he looked on, rubbed her hands over her clean-shaven cunt.

It felt so good to touch herself there. The skin was so soft, so swollen with her need for him. She tugged her lips, letting him watch. For a third time, she put her hands in the slot and rubbed her slippery hands together. With a very naughty smile, she approached him as he sat on the seat. He sighed as her hands danced over the skin of his chest. She knew it was making him ache for her. His cock lengthened as she played with him, begging her to touch it and finally she grabbed hold of it with her soapy hands and gave him the rhythm she knew he craved. Up and down, up and down. Jude put his hands over hers and together they took up the rhythm until with a yell he came, the precious fluid covering their joined hands. Even without their thoughts being joined, Delia knew this was not her vision. It was with someone else, someone equally dear to him but it wasn't her. She knew that no matter who this other person was, she and Jude had something special and enduring. She just needed to make sure he understood that.

Taking the hand sprayer, Delia washed the two of them and returned it to its holder.

"Thank you for that," he said drawing her into his arms and holding her close. Stepping away, he got out of the shower chamber and walked to the wall opposite the shower. "Chamber Seven, two towels," he said and a door opened and a shelf slid out bearing two towels. Unfolding one, he wrapped it around her. She snuggled into it as she realized it was warm. "Another feature my navigator added," he explained. "The cupboard is designed to heat the towels as soon as the shower chamber is activated so there are always warm towels when you finish."

"I think I'd like to meet this navigator of yours someday," she said sleepily.

"Oh, you will. You definitely will," Jude assured her. She had no idea how true those words were.

"I'd also like to try out Number Two and Number Five," she said coquettishly. Jude looked at her, not understanding.

"Number Two and Number Five?" he asked.

"We tried out all the numbers from One to Seven in the shower chamber except for Number Two and Number Five so I want to make sure we try them out next time." Jude laughed.

"We can certainly try them out next time," Jude assured her but in his heart he doubted very much that there would be a next time. He took the second towel and dried himself, watching Delia as she rubbed her body with the warm towel.

"Is it my imagination or is the floor warm as well?" she quizzed.

"Yes. Toryn even thought of that too," he replied.

"Toryn. That's your navigator?"

"Yes" was the brusque reply. *Shields up! Don't give anything away!*

Delia felt the barricade slip firmly into place but not before he let slip that little piece of information. Jude swept her into his arms and carried her back to the bed.

"I don't know about you but I really need to catch a few hours' sleep," he said as he set her down and crawled in beside her.

"That sounds wonderful," Delia said as she snuggled back against him.

Chapter Five

ꟹ

Delia knew she was alone as soon as she awoke. The space beside her was empty, his essence weak, not overpowering like before. Whatever was going to happen was at hand but she knew better than to fight the Fates. Throwing back the covers, she stood by the bed. Lying across the end of the bed was an armored flight suit and some small knives. What a thoughtful man to leave her the weapons of her choice! The flight suit fit like a glove and she felt better knowing she was armed and protected by the light battle armor in the suit. Crossing to the door, it opened instantly, letting her out onto a long corridor that led to a set of elevators. Upon entering the elevators, a voice quietly asked for her destination. Assuming Jude had gone to the bridge that was the destination she chose. The doors opened soundlessly seconds later, allowing her to view the ship's controls with Jude in the captain's chair.

"Come in," he called without turning around. He knew the instant she had woken from her sleep. Their connection was too strong to allow otherwise. "Come and look out," he encouraged. Delia strode forward, ready to embrace whatever happened. As she stood looking out the forward window bay, Jude reached out and pulled her into his lap.

Laughing, Delia said, "Captain, I don't think that's proper military behavior."

"To Panton with proper military behavior!" he retorted. "I want to hold you and since there's no one here but you and me, I can do as I wish." Delia nestled against him, wishing she could see into their future.

"Do you recognize that planet?" he asked as the triple rings came into view. Delia's face lit up as she saw the planet out the window bay.

"It's Tantor!" she said excitedly. "Are we going to visit King Feldan? Do you have business with him?" At Jude's nod she continued. "He and my father are close friends. I didn't know you knew him," she said, turning in his lap to look at him.

"I need to see him about a very important matter and I thought you might like to come along." Delia tried to figure out what was going on. For some reason he knew that she was friends with the king and he needed her to be on the planet with him. So be it. They would go down together. "Let's go to the pod bay and we can grab a speederpod to get to Slidaron."

"Is King Feldan at the castle in Slidaron? I thought he was away with his wife to see their new grandchild."

"Something came up and he had to return. He asked if I would come and help him out." Taking her hand, he led her to the elevator that whisked them silently to the pod bay. As they climbed into the pod he turned to her and said, "Can you fly one of these things if there was an emergency?"

"Of course I can." *What an odd question.*

"Just curious," Jude said. Delia knew he was more than curious but she let it go.

They flew through the sky, the little speeder pod responsive to his slightest touch. The landing bay was eerily silent as they touched down. Usually the area was full of creatures from many different planets, the air filled with the sound of voices and engines and cargo being loaded and unloaded but today there was no sound, just the quiet hum of the speeder pod as it gently settled down. Jude knew she could sense the wrongness of everything around them but he was powerless to stop the plan. The wheels were already in motion.

As they stepped out of the little pod, Jude took her hand, not caring that it wasn't proper protocol. He wanted to have these last few minutes with her. It was obvious that they were expected, the palace guards moving quickly to open massive doors and allow them entry. The very corridors of the palace lacked their normal hustle and bustle. Servants were nowhere to be seen and the usual cacophony of sounds and mélange of smells seemed strangely absent. They paused at a set of gigantic bronze doors that Delia recognized well, their surface an intricate maze of dragons taken from some Old Earth story King Feldan loved. Jude pulled her into his arms and kissed her. "I love you," he whispered as he flung open the towering portals and ushered her inside. The doors flew shut with an ominous thud, leaving them standing inside the massive throne room. King Feldan stood by his throne, his hand gripping one arm of the ornate seat of power. Many times Delia had stood before this throne, welcomed by the man who was like an uncle to her. She had even sat in it as a child, sharing it with King Feldan's daughter, as her father and the king had discussed matters of state.

Delia bowed. Friend or not, he was still king. King Feldan stood unmoving, silent.

"Are you all right?" she asked, concerned by his lack of response.

"Oh, he's just fine," replied a voice from the shadows. A chill spilled through her. She knew that voice, knew what it meant. She had been betrayed.

"Hello, Brachan," she said, hoping her face didn't show the anguish she felt at having been delivered into the hands of her enemy. Turning to the king, she said, "I don't understand."

"He has my daughter. If I didn't cooperate, he would kill her. Many of us are bound to this creature in ways you couldn't imagine. Just remember that!"

"Your job is done," Brachan spat. "Leave us!" With a last look at Delia, King Feldan turned and slowly left the room. Brachan moved from the shadows, his green skin resplendent in the light from the chandeliers. He drew back his pudgy lips in what Delia assumed was a smile and ran a claw down her face, scratching her delicate skin. At the trickle of blood that oozed from the thin cut, Jude shot forward.

"You said you wouldn't hurt her," he cried.

"Come now, Captain. Even you couldn't be so stupid as to think I wouldn't take my revenge. This woman stole from me, lied to me and I demand retribution."

"You were going to torture and kill your wife. I only did what I had to do. I had no choice but to save her."

"She had outlived her usefulness but no matter. You must face the consequences. You will take my wife's place…in all ways." Delia recoiled from the unholy gleam in his bright orange eyes. She would rather be dead than lie with this creature and she was fairly certain that no matter what occurred, death would be the end result and it would be as prolonged and as painful as only a monster such as Brachan could administer.

Turning to Jude, Brachan spoke. "And to show you, Captain, that I am a creature of my word, I will fulfill our bargain. Guards!" A small door opened to the right of the throne and two burly guards appeared, dragging a naked man between them. Coming to a halt in front of their commander, they threw the man to the floor at Brachan's command and marched from the room. Delia looked on as Jude knelt by the wounded man. It was obvious from the bruises covering his massive body that he had been badly beaten but it was also obvious that he was a very handsome man. For some reason, Brachan's thugs hadn't touched his face and he had a striking beauty about him.

"Our bargain has been fulfilled," Brachan said. "Take him and get out!"

"What about her?" Jude asked, looking at Delia.

"Her fate is none of your concern," Brachan shouted. "Just get out!"

Jude tried frantically to communicate with her to let her know it was going to be all right but she was so stricken by his betrayal that she had thrown up her shields and refused to communicate with him. With a last look at Delia, Jude took hold of his wounded comrade and, thanks to his implants, threw him over his shoulder as if he were a child. She watched in silence as he strode to the bronze doors and pulled one open. They slammed shut behind him, leaving her alone with her fate and with Brachan.

"That was the mysterious navigator, I assume?" she said, turning to her captor.

"Yes, that was Toryn. Even wounded he is unbelievably beautiful. Beautiful, strong and cunning. His captain too. Just the way I like them. One can't help but admire the captain's loyalty even if it did mean your betrayal. Amazing what people will do in the name of friendship, isn't it?" Brachan said, shaking his large reptilian head.

"I guess that's something you'll never have to worry about," Delia murmured sarcastically.

"Shut up!" he yelled, striking her across the face, his scales leaving vivid marks. Delia could taste the blood welling in her mouth. She wasn't going down without a fight but she would bide her time. Striking in anger may work for him but she needed to plan better than that.

"Well, if you're going to take my wife's place then I want to see my part of the bargain. Take your clothes off so I can see what I'm getting before I fuck you. Have you ever had a Redelian warrior fuck you before? Trust me. It will be something you'll never forget. I'll make sure of that," he said, laughing malevolently. "I hate fucking humans but I'm going to love sticking my great, big green prong inside you. I hope the barbs on it don't cut you too badly inside but I don't really care. Redelians consider blood to be an aphrodisiac so you may find our lovemaking to be a bit, shall we say, savage." He threw back his head and roared with vicious laughter. "Don't worry though, my healers will stitch you up, put you in the regeneration chamber and in a few hours you will be as you were. By then I'll have steeled myself to having to take you again. Did I tell you that my prong is ten inches long? It can reach deep, deep inside you. I can hardly wait." Delia wasn't sure whether she was going to faint or throw up. She knew Brachan wouldn't care. He'd just wait until she came around then he'd lance her again with his barbarous prong.

Oh great Jobin! How could Jude have abandoned her to such a horrible fate? He had certainly done a number on her. It was all a clever ruse to rescue Toryn and she was the pawn in the game.

"Perhaps you'd like to see my lance of love?" he inquired mockingly, pulling her back to reality. Raising himself to his full height of seven feet, he pulled apart the front closure of his breeches and, from a luxuriant mane of long chartreuse-colored hair, he took out his prong. Delia recoiled at the sight of it. The length and breadth of it was incredible. It was, as he said, ten inches long and now she saw that it was a hideous shade of green. The head of it was the size of her fist and she knew it would tear her apart as he entered her. All down the length of it were rows of barbs that would tear her to pieces as he pulled out of her. No wonder his wife had pleaded with Delia to kill her. Delia couldn't imagine having that thing inside you then being healed in the regeneration chamber just to allow him to do it again and again. She had stolen Mariella from under Brachan's nose and taken her to safety on a distant planet only because Mariella had sought her aid. Now that she knew the horrible truth she was glad she had done it even if it meant her own demise.

Shoving his weapon back into his breeches, Brachan strode regally to the throne and climbed the dais, claiming the royal seat as if it were his own.

"Enough delay! Take off your clothes!" Brachan shouted.

Delia undid the zipper across her breasts then remembered that Jude had left no underclothing for her. As soon as she removed the suit, she would be totally, wholly naked for this beast. She cringed at the thought of having this creature view her nude body. Whether he wanted her or not, he was still going to torture her by fucking her with that hideous rod so the longer she kept her clothes on the better. Brachan stepped down from the throne and crossed to her. He reached up with his clawed hands, grabbed the neck of her suit and ripped it to the waist, exposing her beautiful breasts.

"I suspect if I were a male of your species, I would find you attractive but you are just a fuck-toy to me," he snarled.

Delia refused to grab the tattered suit or to beg for mercy from this brute. She knew that was what he wanted her to do and she also knew it would be futile as he had no intention of letting her live.

"Turn around," he yelled. "I don't wish to see your ugly human face." Delia turned away from him and, kneeling behind her, he tore the suit from her body, leaving her naked and vulnerable.

"I'll just take these," he said with a grin, removing her hidden blades and flinging them across the assembly hall. Without those blades, she really was defenseless although she knew they probably would have been useless against his tough armored hide. They would only have served to make him more angry and she certainly didn't want that. "Turn around so I can see what I'm going to fuck," he commanded. Delia knew that there was little she could do. A tear rolled down her cheek as she thought of her lovemaking with Jude. It had been so precious to her. This animal would use her as a fuck-vessel then discard her until she healed so he could use her again and again. She hoped he would tire of her quickly and kill her.

Turning to meet her fate, she stood proud and tall before the savage beast. He cruelly raked her with his eyes, tracing down her body at the same time with one razor-sharp claw, leaving a thin line of blood trickling from the cut. He cut a thin line between her breasts but Delia refused to flinch or draw back. Something akin to respect shone in Brachan's eyes as he realized this human woman was indeed a worthy opponent. He slit a fine line down her torso to her belly then froze as he reached her pubis.

"Aaaarggg!" he roared, looking at her naked pubis. "Who did this to you?" he howled. "Who has desecrated you in this way?"

Delia had no idea what he was talking about. What did he mean? Then she knew that Jude had saved her. This creature was appalled by her shaved cunt.

"No one has done this to me. This is the fashion on my planet. All women are clean-shaven as I am," she lied to him.

"It was bad enough having to force myself between your legs but to look on that hideous monstrosity exposed by its lack of fur… I won't have it! How dare you appear before me in such a state, you *hieden*."

Before Delia could react to his ferocious anger and move away, he began to attack her with his claws, tearing at her delicate skin. Brachan threw out his arm and backhanded her, forcing her to her knees. The sight of her shaven pubis was so repellent to him, so repellent to his entire race that he had to put aside his vengeance. He would be unable to force himself to put his prong inside that abhorrent flesh.

"Guards," he called, "come and get this *hieden* out of my sight." The last thing Delia saw before she lost consciousness was the same two burly guards who had hauled away Toryn, reaching down to take hold of her. The last thing she heard was Jude's voice in her head. *Trust me, Delia. Trust me.*

Chapter Six

ℌ

It was the hardest thing he had ever done but Jude turned his back on her and walked away. He knew Toryn wouldn't survive if they didn't get him back to the ship pronto. Jude could feel his life force slipping away even as he hauled him through the massive doors. Once the doors had swung shut behind them, Jude gently lay Toryn down on the floor and signaled the waiting speederpod. It had been hidden in an area behind the palace, the crew awaiting Jude's communication to come and retrieve the stricken navigator. Within minutes, the pod arrived, small enough to skim through the wide corridors of the palace with the aid of the onboard compugram. Removing the transpod, Jude gently lowered his friend to the device and floated it to the cradle in the pod where the waiting crew set the holding beams to secure Toryn in. Jude knew that as soon as they got to *The Renegade,* the medics on board would put him into the neurocharger and its healing rays would instantly repair any damage to his body. He also knew that speed was of the essence for although the neurocharger could heal any degree of damage from light to severe, it was incapable of resuscitating someone who was already dead. The pod would rendezvous with *The Renegade* within minutes and the mini-neurocharger aboard the little transport vessel would sustain Toryn until they reached the ship. Now all Jude had to do was wait.

No sound penetrated the heavy bronze doors so he let down his shields to probe her thoughts but she was so angry with him that she blocked his every effort. He had no idea what was happening to Delia. He knew his plan was a good one, albeit a little offbeat but he had studied enough about Brachan to know how he would react to her little surprise.

Happily he had never seen a naked Redelian but the stories he had heard told of long, luxuriant pubic hair of which the vile creatures were inordinately proud. He expected Brachan to be no different. It seemed like the ultimate antithesis on such a reptilian-like creature but if that little idiosyncrasy was able to save Delia's life then he would use it. In fact, her life depended on Brachan being repulsed by her shaved cunt. He just hoped Brachan didn't kill her in his anger. Jude knew that was a very real possibility.

All at once he felt the veil lift from his mind and knew that she was slipping away. He was panicked, worried that he'd left it too long. *Trust me, Delia. Trust me.* He hoped his words would force her to hang on.

Suddenly the massive bronze doors swung open and the same two brawny guards appeared, this time with Delia slung between them. Lifting her high in their arms, they threw her forward, letting her collapse at Jude's feet. "Brachan says to take your garbage home. If it lives," they added with a laugh. Jude fell to the floor, taking her in his arms, the crude guards forgotten. His scanners told him that she was still alive, barely. Frantically he hailed the speederpod, relieved to discover that it was already on its way back. He shouldn't have doubted his crew, they knew the plan. The small craft appeared down the long hallway, the crew stepping out almost before it came to a stop. They knew their captain would be beside himself to get her to the neurocharger before it was too late. Jude climbed in beside her, conscious of the fact that this seemed all too familiar. The difference was the last time she was just a woman he needed for his plan, this time she was a woman he needed to survive.

When they got to *The Renegade,* Jude hovered until the medics finally told him she and Toryn were going to be fine and to go away. He went off in a huff, knowing that they would need to sleep for several hours after spending time in the neurocharger. It was the body's way of helping with the healing process. Making his way back to his cabin, he threw off his clothes and lay down on the bed, aware that neither Delia nor Toryn would be released from sick bay for a few hours but when they were they would be hale and hearty and healed.

He really didn't mean to sleep but his body had other ideas and he drifted off almost immediately. He was awakened a little while later by a delightful tongue making its way down his chest.

"Delia," he whispered.

"No," came the laughing reply in a deep masculine voice. "Were you hoping it was?" Now the tongue covered his nipple and flicked it gently. Jude opened his eyes to see the beautiful face of his navigator hovering there. "Thank you for coming to get me," Toryn said. "I didn't think I was going to make it."

Jude reached up and caressed his cheek. "I thought that you were just my navigator and sometimes lover but I realized that it was more than that," he said. "But now I have a problem."

"I know. You need *her* too." Toryn had had a lot of time to think while Brachan held him captive. He had been certain that Jude would rescue him but he also knew that although he and his captain had only made love a few times, he felt more than just lust for him. It was easy to imagine how Jude felt about this woman.

"How do you know about her?" Jude quizzed.

"The whole crew is talking about her but I don't understand how she fits into the story." Jude told him that he had kidnapped Delia for the express purpose of trading her for Toryn but once he had her on the ship, everything had changed. He told him that he was somehow connected to this woman just as he was connected to Toryn.

"I had come up with a plan to rescue you but I couldn't leave her behind either. Can you understand that?"

Toryn leaned down and gently kissed Jude on the mouth, a kiss of gratitude, a kiss of understanding. "The woman is sleeping in the adjoining cabin and won't awaken for some time yet. Her wounds weren't as severe as mine but she's smaller and needs more time to recuperate. Would you like to take a shower while you wait for her to recuperate?"

"With you?" Jude asked with a smile.

"Of course with me."

Jude blessed the day Toryn had forced the captain to take him on as navigator. He was a fabulous navigator and a wonderful lover. As this whole chain of events had unfolded, Jude had come to the realization that he would have gone through the fires of Portulia to rescue Toryn but now he knew Toryn would have done the same for him. Toryn slid off the bed, putting his hand out to draw Jude to his feet. Standing together, it was easy to see that Jude was taller and more muscular than Toryn but Toryn could hold his own in any kind of scrap. He was smaller than Jude's six feet three but at six feet one he still towered over most men. Jude reached out and ran his hands over Toryn's chest, just delighted to have him back and in one piece.

"I missed you," he said, "and I worried that you were already dead." Looking down at Toryn's enormous erection, he smiled and said, "I missed that too."

Reaching forward, he put his hands on both sides of Toryn's head and gently kissed his eyes, his cheeks, his succulent lips. He used his tongue to trace his navigator's bottom lip then nipped along it before he thrust his tongue inside his mouth. Toryn responded to the feel of Jude's tongue in his mouth, tracing along the inside of his cheeks, across his sensitive palate. It seemed like so long since they had been together.

"He didn't hurt you, did he?" Jude asked, concern in his voice.

"Not in the way you mean," Toryn replied. "He is definitely only interested in the female of any species. He took delight in beating me or having his thugs torture me but he wasn't interested in fucking me."

"Let's see if I can help you forget what he did to you," Jude said as he took Toryn by the hand and led him to the shower chamber. As soon as they entered, Toryn pulled up short.

"What is it?" Jude asked.

"I can smell what you did in here with her. It smells delicious. Does she taste good?" Toryn asked curiously.

"She tastes exquisite," Jude replied. "Would you like to pleasure her with me?" Jude knew that Toryn had never made love with a woman before.

"I think I would like to pleasure her together. Do you think she would like that?"

"We'll just have to wait and ask her," Jude responded.

* * * * *

Delia came awake with a start, expecting to feel unbearable pain, expecting to see that repulsive creature staring at her. Instead she felt Jude close by and knew that she was safe. Remembering what Brachan had done to her, she pushed the sheet down to see how damaged her body was and was amazed to find not a mark on her. All her terrible wounds were healed and not a scar remained as a testament to her terrible ordeal.

She didn't know how long she'd been sleeping but she did know that now that she was awake, nature called and she called urgently. Gingerly swinging her legs over the side of the bed, she was startled to find that she was sure and steady on her feet as if her nightmare with Brachan had never taken place. Whatever magic the medics of *The Renegade* had worked on her, she was very grateful. Looking around the unfamiliar cabin, she realized that it was not Jude's cabin but she could feel him close by. His screens were down and totally inactive as if he no longer needed them. Suddenly she was slammed with unbearable lust, waves of it flowing through her body like a firestorm. Without the barrier to his thoughts in place, she was bombarded with his feelings. Stumbling around the room, she passed through an open door to find herself in a small bathroom. This bathroom was a basic, serviceable room for performing the necessary functions and nothing more. There was no elaborate shower chamber with multiple showerheads, no warming cupboard with fresh, warm towels inside and no array of seats in the shower chamber.

After making use of the facilities, Delia grabbed a robe someone had left at the foot of the bed and went in search of Jude. Stepping out into the passageway, she saw that she had been given the cabin next to his. As she stood at his door wondering how to get in, it slid open soundlessly. Delia didn't know that Jude had programmed the door to recognize her DNA so it accepted her instantly and allowed her entry.

As she stepped over the threshold, the hunger was so strong it raised the fine hairs on the back of her neck with its ferocity. Heading toward the elaborate bathroom, she could feel the waves of lust pulsing in the air. They were so intense she felt like she should be able to reach out and touch them. Stepping into the bathroom, she stopped just inside the door and saw the two of them together in the shower chamber. They were so beautiful together that she wanted to cry out to them. Jude was taller than Toryn but both were covered in heavy muscle. It was obvious that they worked hard for a living. They were broad through the shoulders, their bodies tapering to abs that had not an ounce of fat on them, then lean through the hips and long in the cock. It was difficult not to stare at them.

As Delia watched, Jude put his hands into the soap dispenser then rubbed them together. He put his slippery hands to Toryn's chest, lovingly caressing him and playing with his stiff little nipples. Delia could feel those hands caressing her breasts at the same time. Every stroke across Toryn's broad chest was mirrored across her breasts. Each time

Jude tugged on Toryn's nipples or pinched them gently, her nipples felt the companion pull. She watched, enraptured, as he gently pushed Toryn back until he was at the seat she had sat on. Toryn reached up and grabbed the vertical bars, lifting himself onto the seat. It was evident that they had done this before and now Delia knew who was in her vision with Jude, it was Toryn.

From this level, Jude was able to lean forward and nibble on Toryn's belly, licking each little bite with his strong tongue. Toryn's enormous erection stood strong and proud, each touch of Jude's cheek against it making it lengthen and swell until Toryn felt like his skin was too tight. Jude put his tongue to the little slit in the tip of Toryn's massive shaft and licked the little drop of pre-cum.

Delia felt Jude's tongue poking up under her clit, nudging the little nub to attention. As he grabbed his navigator's cock and slid it into his mouth, Delia put her hand between her legs and began to tease the little button of flesh hidden there. Her body could feel Jude's mouth sucking the big cock yet it also felt her own hand circling her clit, drawing it out. She watched as Jude applied suction with his cheeks and tongue and felt Toryn so close to the edge. Jude began to move his head up and down Toryn's penis, grabbing tighter and tighter with his mouth and running his tongue up and down, feeling the heavy veins running the length of the huge cock. Delia began to press harder on her clit, flattening it out, seeking the secret center, the point of the most pleasure. She could feel Toryn's orgasm bubbling to the surface like hot lava and with a rush she exploded with him, tremors racking her frame. Their combined orgasm went on and on, shaking her body with its ferocity. She could see that Toryn was shaking as well. Did he realize that her orgasm had become a part of him?

Toryn slowly slid down from the seat, advancing on his lover and turning him to face the wall. Delia realized they were by one of the showerheads she and Jude hadn't used. Of course Toryn knew all the intricacies of the shower system. He had designed it, so maybe she would get to see what kind of pleasure that showerhead would bring. She didn't have long to wait. Toryn took Jude's hands and placed them flat on the wall in front of him.

Delia realized she was holding her breath in anticipation. She watched as Toryn reached into the soap dispenser and got some lather on his hands. First he used the rich foam to wash Jude's back then as she looked on he slid his hand down Jude's back, fingers first and put his long middle finger to the little puckered hole in Jude's backside. Oh great Panton! Delia knew what that was going to feel like. Jude had done that to her. She shivered as she felt his finger penetrate them, stretching the tight skin to allow entry. She watched as he gently drove it in and out of Jude's body. He was driving it in and out of Jude's body but she could feel it in her butt as well. In, out, in, out, a river of pleasure pouring over them.

Toryn put his hand back into the dispenser but this time he grabbed his erection and lathered it. Delia squirmed as she now knew what a man felt with his hands on himself. He was so hard and so warm. The skin was soft and smooth but his cock was so hard, the veins bulging as it beat in time with his pulse. He must have called to the showerhead by the high seat, for the water came on for an instant to let him wash the soap from his hands then he put his hand into the compartment where Jude had found the shaving cream. His hand was shiny as he put his fingers again to Jude's tight hole. Delia realized it was lubricant and he was making it easier for him to enter.

Using the rest of the lube on his own cock, Toryn grabbed his hard-on and began to spread Jude's tiny hole. Delia gasped as it began to enter her, the pain unbearable as he stretched her to the limit. She heard Jude cry out at the unbelievable pleasure then Toryn was past the rosette and pushing his way inside. He was huge inside them, his cock pushing against their inner walls, exerting incredible pressure. Just when she thought the exquisite torture couldn't become any more intense, he began to move. Toryn reached around Jude and grabbed his cock, jacking him off at the same time. He called to the showerhead that was mounted on the wall between Jude's legs and as he pulled on his lover's penis the water began to pulse a rhythm that hit Jude right in the balls.

It was too much for Delia. Toryn went off first, exploding into Jude then Delia felt herself quiver into release. Jude let go of the wall with one hand and placed it on top of Toryn's and together they brought him to completion, his fluid running over their hands, Delia's vision come to life. Delia didn't have the strength to stand and watch them shower off the residue from their lovemaking. Turning, she made her way to her cabin where she threw the robe on the bed and crawled in, falling into a sleep of exhaustion.

"Do you think she realized that we knew she was there?" Toryn asked as he stood leaning into Jude's body. Jude shook his head.

"She knew she was part of our feelings but forgot that we were sharing hers too."

"That was pretty intense," Toryn said, stating the obvious. "I've never had sex with a woman's point of view involved and I loved it. Her connection with us was so strong. I just wish one of us had been inside her so I could feel what it's like inside a woman. How do you think she felt about us making love?"

"I'd say she loved it." Stepping out of the shower chamber, Jude grabbed two warm towels from the hidden armoire. Handing one to Toryn, he kissed him deeply then began to dry off. "Will you come to my bed now?" Jude asked him.

"I need to be with you," Toryn replied.

"Would you like me to go get Delia and put her in my bed so she'll be with us when she wakes up? I can feel that she's fallen asleep already so we can do it without waking her."

"Yes, I'd like to wake up with her between us," Toryn said with a mischievous grin. "Maybe she'll let us make love to her." Toryn found he was very curious about this woman.

"I certainly hope so," Jude replied as he padded across the bedroom to go bring her in. Delia hadn't noticed that their cabins had a connecting door so Jude didn't have to go out in the passageway to fetch her. As he stood watching her sleep, he felt Toryn come and stand beside him.

"She's so beautiful," Jude said, "but strong and feisty too and a good fighter. She would make a great bounty hunter. No one would ever suspect a beautiful woman like that of being a bounty hunter. The three of us would be an incredible team."

"I suspect she'd be good in any role she chooses. I think we definitely need her with us," Toryn said. He looked on as Jude gently picked her up and carried her to the bed in the captain's cabin. Toryn grabbed the robe from her bed and threw it at the foot of Jude's. When she woke and found herself in bed with the two of them, she just might want it. He crawled in at her front and Jude spooned her body from the back and they fell asleep, eager to see what happened when she awoke cradled between them.

Chapter Seven

ဢ

As Delia woke to feel Jude slide his great hard cock into her from behind, she knew she was right where she belonged. Keeping her eyes closed to savor the closeness, she eased her free arm around him while he leisurely slid in and out of her weeping channel. Nothing felt as good as this man's cock surging in then sliding out of her welcoming body, touching her heart and her body as no man had ever done.

Running her hand down his powerful torso, she rubbed the very tip of one tight, little nipple with the flat of her finger, drew a lazy circle inside his belly button, finally coming to rest on his hefty erection. A man's penis was such a dichotomy with its sensitive head and the baby-soft skin covering the iron-hard pleasure within. She ran her forefinger over the tip, smoothing the little drop around the silky, smooth crown then traced the sizeable length with her finger, bringing it back up to paint a line under the collar. She heard him gasp as she took hold of him and squeezed very gently. With a predictable reaction, she felt him swell in her hands, his life force pounding through the bulging veins. Opening her eyes, she saw that the cabin was shadowed in darkness, the only light coming from a small lamp across the room. She felt like she was in a dream, a warm, erotic dream, hazy with the smell of lust and love in the air. Oh, how she loved being with this man.

Leaning forward, she bit him on the shoulder, grinning as he started then licking to soothe the sting. Then she nuzzled his neck, turning her head to take a tiny nip of his earlobe. His cock jumped in response, indicating its approval. Tightening her hold on his cock, she planted a row of featherlight kisses along his shoulder, his long, soft hair tickling her face.

Toryn wondered when she was going to realize that it was his erection she was fondling not Jude's but until that happened his cock was going to enjoy all the attention she was lavishing on it.

Delia petted his cock as he deepened the rhythm and began to pound into her. The air was filled with the sound of his flesh slapping her butt, her moans lifting above them. She took the tempo with her hand and ran it up and down his cock, a race to see who would finish first. With a guttural cry, he erupted over her hand, his hips jerking with the force. A few more pounding strokes and Delia followed him, yelling her release in his ear.

Jude and Toryn waited to see her reaction. They had kept their screens up so she wouldn't realize they were both with her. Jude hoped that wouldn't make her angry.

Delia wasn't sure what made her realize that something was odd. Perhaps it was when she noticed that she was holding a cock with one already firmly embedded inside her. She knew it was Jude inside her, her body and her heart told her. Bending forward, she gave Toryn a sharp bite on the shoulder. At his jump she laughed.

"Toryn, I presume," she said. Toryn turned around so he could look at her.

"At your service," he said, a trace of laughter in his voice.

"Oh, I certainly hope so," Delia replied.

"I hope you don't mind waking up in bed with the two of us," Toryn continued.

"Why didn't you say something when I started to touch you?" Delia asked.

"I've never made love with a woman before but I loved having your hands on me. I didn't realize how different the touch of a woman would be, more gentle, softer."

"You've never made love with a woman before?" Delia asked, surprised.

"When I was growing up, I knew it was men that I was destined to be with and on my home planet that is normal, accepted. No one is looked down on for their sexual preferences so I've only ever made love with other men."

"Would you like to make love with a woman?" she asked, unsure of her own reaction to that question.

"I loved the connection of you touching me with Jude deep inside you at the same time. I'd like to make love with you, with you and Jude, if you'd like."

Delia was quiet, thinking about making love with the two of them.

Jude spoke softly from behind her. "We wanted you to wake up with us. I wasn't very honest with you before so I wanted to let you see the truth."

Delia knew there were things that needed to be brought out in the open so she softly said, "I thought you had betrayed me to that monster."

"I'll be honest with you now," Jude said, gently running his fingers through her hair. "When I heard that Brachan had placed a bounty on your head, I saw that as a way to get Toryn back. It seemed so easy. After all, I'm a bounty hunter. The plan was very simple—kidnap you, turn you over to Brachan, Toryn gets released." Toryn took over the telling.

"Then he met you and everything changed. His simple plan was no longer simple. He was in a terrible dilemma, needing to rescue me but not wanting to lose you. So he came up with Plan B. Bounty hunters always have a Plan B which usually means Plan A has failed miserably and you need to somehow find a way out of the clusterfuck you've created." Delia laughed. Toryn reached out and stroked her face. "He fell for you, in a big way, and needed an alternate plan."

"You figured out the alternate plan, didn't you?" Jude asked hesitantly. She nodded.

"How did you know that about Brachan, about the Redelians?" Delia demanded. "How could you put my life on the line like that? He was so angry I thought he was going to kill me."

"I had no idea he would be so furious. From the stories I had heard, I figured he would be repulsed then just throw you out."

"Well, he did that but not before he made sure I knew how angry he was."

"I'm sorry he hurt you. That wasn't part of the plan. I hope you can forgive me. I was just trying to save the two people I care about most." Delia looked at Toryn who was watching her intently, waiting for her reply. She could see his feelings for Jude and realized how difficult it must have been for Jude to decide how to save them both. There was only one thing to say.

"My answer is yes," she said. Jude heaved a sigh of relief.

"Yes, you forgive me?" She shook her head. Jude frowned.

"Yes, I want to make love with both of you." Jude knew she had forgiven him. Delia watched the smile on Toryn's face turn from one of joy to one of intent. Now that she had agreed to make love with the two of them she could see that Toryn was eager to get started.

"I'm just going to use the bathroom," she said nervously, needing a bit of space. Before she could get out of bed, Jude reached to the bottom of the bed and handed her the robe. She was grateful for his thoughtfulness and shyly got out of bed and put it on.

As Delia disappeared into the bathroom, Toryn propped the pillows behind him and sat up in bed. Looking down at Jude, he asked, "Do you think she regrets her decision to make love with us?"

Jude shook his head. "No. I think it's like trying anything you haven't tried before. There's always that nervousness about it and this is something totally outside her realm of experience. I think we just need to take it slow and easy and let it happen." Toryn looked down at him.

"My greatest fear while I lay in my cell waiting for you to come and rescue me was that it would be too late and I would die without seeing you again." Putting out his hand, he ran it down his lover's face. Delia stood just inside the bathroom door, listening to them talk. She knew she loved Jude but what was happening between Jude and Toryn was strong enough to include her too. As she came back into the room, Toryn and Jude were surprised to see her smiling at them, no hesitation about what they were going to do.

"I've never done anything like this before," she said. "I don't know where to begin."

Jude opened his arms to her, saying, "We've never had anyone else with us either so we'll get to experiment together."

"I don't know if I want to do this without my screens in place," Delia said. "I think it might be too much for me the first time. I think I'd like to try it as just me." Jude and Toryn nodded in agreement and wordlessly put up their screens. As Toryn lay against the pillows watching, Jude pushed back the covers and climbed out of bed.

"Are you feeling better today?" he asked, running his hands, palms out, down the inside of the satin lapels of the robe. She nodded, shivering as his knuckles rubbed her sensitive nipples. "You certainly feel good," he said, leaning forward to trace her lips with his tongue then kissing her deeply. As he kissed her, he continued to rub his knuckles up and down over her nipples until they were as hard as little *pingles.* Breaking the kiss, he untied her robe and pulled it off her shoulders, letting it fall to the floor. Now he rubbed his knuckles over her breasts without the robe to mask any of the pleasure. Using his thumb and forefinger, he took hold of her long nipples, gently pulling then pinching them.

Toryn lay watching, his eager cock tenting the bedclothes. He'd been afraid that he would hate to see Jude making love with someone else but the truth was that he loved it, was turned on by it. Climbing out of bed, he stood behind Jude and ran his hands over his lover's butt cheeks then up his sculpted back. Reaching under his arms, he forged a sensuous path to Jude's massive chest where he sought his lover's tender nipples. With his middle fingers, he rubbed lightly back and forth across the ultra-sensitive buds then pulled and pinched them as Jude was doing to Delia. Even with their screens up such an intense experience was divine torture.

Toryn looked on as Jude took Delia by the waist and turned her away from him so he could trace her graceful spine, with his tongue. As the captain leaned forward, Toryn dragged his hands away from Jude's chest so he could trace down his comrade's spine with his middle finger, touching each bone on his journey until his finger ran down the crease of Jude's ass. Stepping away, he grabbed some lubricant from the drawer of the bedside table and squirted it into his hand. Throwing the tube onto the bed, he covered his rod with the lube then put some on Jude's little hole. He grabbed his friend by the hips and eased his cock inside.

Delia heard Jude moan then felt his hands grasp her tighter then fall away completely. She turned to see his head thrown back in ecstasy, passion etched in every line of his face. Knowing what she was going to see, she went behind him and watched as Toryn's huge cock nudged its way inside. She couldn't look away as the beautiful men made love. The massive cock disappeared little by little into his channel until Toryn's pubic hair almost touched Jude's cheeks. Jude grabbed a nearby chair so he could lean over comfortably and Toryn began to press gently in then pull out. Delia moved back in front of Jude and knelt between him and the chair. As Toryn pleasured him from the back, she reached up and took hold of Jude's hard-on, licking the crest first then around the collar then down the shaft. He howled and no wonder with the double pleasure of two lovers. Delia opened her mouth wide, letting Jude's cock slide inside. As Toryn increased the pace and began to pump into him from the back she applied pressure with her cheeks from the front.

Jude thought his head was going to explode. Thank Jobin he'd activated his screens. He knew it would have been too much to be connected as three. Feeling it just as one was intense enough with Toryn thrusting into him from the back and Delia's voracious mouth gobbling him from the front. Making love as three was incredible. Making love with the two people you love most was incredible. He didn't know whether to focus on the delight of her tongue rimming the head of his cock then sliding down the turgid length or to focus on the heavy iron bar jackhammering from the back.

Toryn's acute senses zeroed in on his cock and the sounds of their lovemaking that broke the quiet of the chamber. Every stroke of his cock into Jude's backside was accompanied by the sounds of flesh meeting flesh, that unmistakable slap of skin-to-skin contact. He heard his sometime lover moan as Delia, their new lover, took Jude in her mouth, the soft, sucking sound of her pleasuring him running along Toryn's nerve endings, tickling his senses and lengthening his cock even more. Toryn caught the sound of Jude's whimper as the captain felt himself being penetrated even more deeply.

"Do you want me to stop?" he said, afraid he was hurting him in his eagerness to please them.

"Never!" Jude said through gritted teeth, unwilling to relinquish even a second of the unbearable pleasure. Satisfied that the whimpers were more from pleasure than from pain, Toryn continued to thrust into Jude's tender hole.

Delia couldn't believe what was happening. Never in her wildest dreams had she ever expected to make love with two men and even if she had thought about it in the dark recesses of her mind, she would never have believed the indescribable ecstasy to be had being with two men at the same time. Even though his screens were in place, that didn't stop her from sharing every quiver and shiver of Jude's body as Toryn pumped into him from behind. It was so erotic to see such gorgeous warriors pleasuring each other. With Jude's cock in her mouth she could feel it pulse in time to each stroke of

Toryn's cock reaching inside him. Grabbing it tighter with her mouth, she moved her head up and down, using her lips to massage the sensitive skin. She felt the changes as his orgasm bubbled to the surface, surging through his veins. His whole body grew taut then with a growl he erupted in her mouth, spewing rivers of hot liquid down her throat. She gobbled it up, swallowing his very essence, using her mouth and lips to milk him dry. Standing up, she looked on as Toryn rose to completion as well.

Putting his arms tightly around Jude allowed him the leverage to pummel his lover with his big, hard cock. She stared as Toryn's cock swung in and out, never quite pulling out of Jude's body. Toryn's body was a work of art, hard and muscular and to watch it pleasuring Jude's rock-hard body was sheer paradise. Suddenly Toryn's body froze, his shaft deep within and Delia watched as he began to shudder as his release came down on him. His eyes fell shut, his neck muscles grew taut, his breathing more rapid and he began to furiously pump into his comrade, giving him every drop of his precious fluid until, spent, he fell against Jude's back.

Delia walked quietly to the bathroom and activating the towel cupboard, removed a heated washcloth. Running the water until warm, she wet the cloth and returned to the lovers. They were frozen as if in a tableau or captured in a Roman statue, two virile warriors joined together in the aftermath of their passion. Delia wished she could draw or paint as the portrait of the rugged, male lovers was worthy of preserving. As she drew close, Toryn gently pulled out of Jude's body and smiled hesitantly at her. Delia knelt at the navigator's feet and returning his smile, carefully wiped away the remnants of their lovemaking.

Toryn watched spellbound as she tenderly wiped his cock then pressed a little kiss to the tip. He realized how different it was making love with a woman. They seemed to be so tender, so caring. He could get used to that. He loved to be with Jude but he was quite sure there was room in his life for this woman as well.

Releasing his hold on the chair, Jude turned to watch Delia gently cleansing Toryn and he smiled. The smile was quickly replaced by a frown when she placed the kiss on his lover's penis.

"Hey! What about me?" he cried. Delia came around behind him and began to wipe his butt cheeks. He pivoted away from her, laughing as she tried to follow him. "I meant what about a kiss for me?" he said, pulling her into his arms. Throwing the washcloth to the floor, Delia put her arms around his neck and drew his face down to hers.

"You mean like this?" she asked flirtatiously, licking across the seam of his lips then thrusting her tongue into his mouth so she could duel with his tongue. It was a kiss of joy. She traced the sensitive skin right behind his top teeth then tickled his palate with her tongue. Judging by the size of the erection pressing against her belly, Jude was definitely enjoying the kiss. Teasingly she pulled her tongue back, hoping he would follow and he did, pressing his tongue into her mouth and flicking just the tip of hers. Delia felt Toryn kneel between them and knew that he must be seeking Jude's gorgeous erection to torment with his mouth. Now instead of Jude's staff rubbing her belly, it was Toryn's soft hair as he ran his tongue up and down Jude's huge cock.

Pulling away from Jude's kiss, she went to her knees between Toryn's spread legs and planted a row of delicate kisses down his spine. While he tongued Jude's massive cock, she put her hands flat on his back and dragged them lightly from his shoulders to his waist. His back was so beautiful, all muscle and sinew, that she couldn't resist nipping along his shoulders. She wanted to bite him. He looked so strong and virile.

Toryn loved the feel of this woman's hands on him. He thought he would weep when she came from the bathroom with the warm washcloth and wiped his genitals. She was so gentle with him as if he were something precious, then when she planted the kiss on his tip, he wanted to burst out of his skin. He had watched Jude's cock lengthen and harden the longer his friend and Delia kissed until he had to step in and put that luscious instrument deep in his mouth. He felt Jude's hands come to rest on his shoulders then, with her first kiss on his backbone, realized that Delia was now kneeling behind him, snuggled between his legs. It felt so good when she kissed a path down his spine he was afraid he might get carried away and bite Jude's cock. Then she trailed her fingers down his back, stopping to nip along his shoulder. He wanted her to bite him. He wanted to put his cock inside her. Rising to his feet, he turned to Delia and held out his hand.

Jude looked on, curious as to what was going through Toryn's mind. It wasn't like Toryn to leave him unfulfilled but the few times they'd been together they'd never had a woman make love with them.

"I'd like to make love with you," he said to Delia, searching her face for acceptance.

"I thought that's what we were doing," she said, taking his hand and letting him pull her to her feet.

"I want to be inside you," he declared. Jude looked on, amazed at what was happening. Toryn had never expressed an interest in making love with a woman. Jude loved women. He loved how different it was making love with them but Toryn appeared content to have only male lovers. That seemed about to change.

Chapter Eight

ꕤ

Jude wasn't quite sure how he felt about that change. He didn't know if it was Toryn he didn't want to share or Delia he didn't want to share. He wasn't quite sure how he felt until he saw the way Toryn was looking at Delia as if she were about to reveal the secrets of the galaxy to him. Having made love with this incredible woman made him realize that she should be the one to introduce Toryn to the mysteries of lovemaking between a man and a woman.

Delia didn't know what to say. Of course she had known that this was going to happen when she decided to make love with the two of them yet it seemed strange thinking about making love but not with Jude. Although she had known him only a short time, she felt a link to him even with their screens in place. Yet Toryn seemed to pull at her body and her heart in the same way. She was probably feeling herself becoming part of the connection forged between the two of them.

"You've really never made love with a woman before," she asked. Toryn shook his head. "Well, that's about to change." Toryn turned to Jude looking for his acceptance. He wasn't sure how Jude would feel about this and he could understand it if Jude felt somewhat possessive of her. After all, he had schemed to keep her from remaining in Brachan's clutches. Moreover he saw the way Jude looked at her. He was relieved when Jude smiled. He watched as Jude went and sat on the bed, propping himself up against the pile of pillows.

Unsure how to proceed, Toryn just stood and stared at Delia. She really was beautiful with her long, dark hair and green eyes. He'd never had a chance to look at a woman's body before and was intrigued by how different it was from a man's. Where a man's body was strong and muscular she was lean and toned. Reaching out to her, he cupped her breasts, filling his hands with their weight. They were heavy but the skin was soft and pliant so unlike Jude's rock-hard chest. Her nipples were large and a delicate shade of brown. He watched them grow long and hard under his intense scrutiny. Reaching up with his thumb and forefinger, he pinched them lightly and was delighted to hear her moan in response.

"Do you like that?" he asked.

"Very much," she said quietly and it was true. Becoming more curious about this female body, he decided that many of the things that would please a man would please a woman so he took a nipple in his mouth. He was unprepared for the rush of pleasure that shook his body. Where Jude's nipples were small and tight to his chest, hers were long and soft against his tongue. He discovered that by taking more of her breast into his mouth he could suck on it as he had once seen a baby do with its mother. Delia took his hand and put it on her other breast then shut her eyes. Toryn understood immediately and began to torment her lonely nipple. Pulling back, he bit down gently and was rewarded with a sigh of delight from Delia. Switching nipples, he began to tug the other nipple with his teeth, not hard enough to hurt but hard enough to tantalize, to tease.

From his spot on the bed, Jude watched Toryn play with Delia's breasts and realized that he enjoyed watching their loveplay. His cock was thick and heavy, lying pulsing on his belly. As much as he wanted to join them, he wanted to let Toryn enjoy his exploration and discovery of Delia's lovely body so he lay back and put his hand on his shaft. Willing her to open her eyes, he watched as she turned her head and saw him cradling his hard-on in his fist.

Wetness pooled between her legs as she lost herself in the tugging of Toryn's teeth while watching Jude run his fist up and down his cock. Leaving her breasts, Toryn set out to kiss a path from her breasts to her belly button. Delia placed her hands on his shoulders, afraid she might melt into a puddle of molten lust at his feet if she didn't.

Through her giggles, Toryn discovered that her navel was a very ticklish spot as he traced it with his tongue. He loved the feel of her soft, warm skin against his lips, so different from the skin of a man's belly. Splaying his fingers on her tummy, he dragged them down her body, stopping at her shaven pubis.

"This is how he saved you, isn't it?" he asked gently. Looking down at him, Delia nodded. "I'm so very glad," he whispered, kissing her softly above her mound. As Jude looked on, Toryn separated her folds with his thumbs and hesitantly put his tongue to her slit. It was as if he was unsure of her taste but he needn't have worried, she was delightful. Putting his tongue up into the little pocket of skin at the top of her crease, Toryn could feel her little nubbin of pleasure and he poked it with his tongue. He hardly had time to react before her warm honey gushed out and he lapped at it with his tongue, greedy for her essence. That was it for Jude. Delia looked over at his harsh cry, just in time to see his luscious cream jet out over his belly. Toryn looked over as well but Delia had to laugh at his reaction.

"What a waste!" was all he said then he got back to the business at hand—or mouth, as the case may be. Returning to Delia's delectable cunt, he determined that he wanted to explore her luscious secret folds, savor all her secret places, discover the mysteries that were woman. He wanted to take his time as he ventured into the unfamiliar world of the female body.

"I want you to climb on the bed so I can look at you but I want to take care of Jude first," he said. Delia smiled and climbed on the bed to wait for him. Picking up the washcloth from the floor, he went to the bathroom and rinsed it out then ran it under warm water again. Returning to the cabin, he strode to the bed and climbed up alongside the captain.

Delia watched his long-legged stride as he crossed the floor to cleanse Jude. His body was like a well-honed machine, no excess fat, all lean muscle. He was well honed and well hung with one particularly large muscle that was starting to grow even larger. She hoped that growth was from thinking about being inside her for she was eager to feel that awe-inspiring flesh driving into her. Now that she had come to terms with making love with two lovers, she was eager to savor both these men. She turned and looked on as Toryn put out his hand to wipe the semen from Jude's belly. She understood when his expression changed as he contemplated that gorgeous cock. She wanted to be him when, throwing the cloth to the floor, he leaned over and began to lap the ambrosia from Jude's taut abdomen. She was afraid that he would forget about her but she needn't have worried for, with a last swipe of his tongue, he turned to her with a wicked gleam in his eye. It was obvious that his cleansing of Jude had only served to whet his appetite and that he was eager for more.

Climbing off the bed, he grabbed her ankles and pulled her to the edge, laughing as she pretended to struggle to get away. He knew she wanted him as much as he wanted her but it was the chase that was exciting to them. He took her legs and tried to spread them apart but she fought to keep them together.

"Let me see your hidden secrets," he purred to her.

"If I let you see my hidden secrets what will be my reward?" she questioned.

"Untold pleasures," he assured her. Jude knew this was the truth. Even though Toryn had never pleasured a woman, he was such a wonderful lover that Jude was sure he would do exactly as he said—bring her untold pleasures and he would get to watch.

As soon as Delia relaxed her legs, Toryn knelt between them and spread her legs, exposing her rosy depths to his gaze. The female of the species was so different. He was elated to discover how different. Between Jude's legs was soft skin yet it covered a cock like an iron bar but between this woman's legs the soft skin was a secret hiding place, fleshy folds that seemed to invite him to delve in and explore. Putting out his hand, he touched her plump lips, investigating their texture, loving how they felt with no hair covering them. Running his finger down the fleshy labia, he was delighted to feel her shiver. He was pleased to know that he made her shiver.

Using his thumbs, he spread her lips to see her entrance dripping with juice. He knew how sweet it would be on his tongue so he inserted the tip of it and sipped her honey. It was like the sweetest nectar. But he wanted more! Pulling himself to his feet, he took her legs and wrapped them around his waist. He was surprised to find how natural the whole thing became to him, knowing exactly what to do. Taking his thick cock in one hand, he closed his eyes and began to nudge it past her lips, feeling them slide over it like silk then her little opening started to swallow him, letting the strong inner muscles grab and guide him inside her. It felt like paradise. The walls of her passage were smooth and strong, gripping him tightly as he pressed inside her channel. He smiled as he felt her tighten and release, hugging his cock then relaxing. When he was fully inside, he stood, just letting the moment be etched in his memory. Then he began to move, slowly at first, savoring the tug of her muscles and the juiciness of her passage. She hugged him like a glove, using her muscles to grab his immense erection and massage it as it slid in and out. He'd thought that nothing could compare with being deep inside another man but he'd never been gripped by the snug channel of a woman's body before and he decided that it was just about the closest he'd ever get to Jobin's paradise.

The dip of the bed apprised him of Jude's movements and he shivered to think that maybe paradise was going to come a lot closer. As he felt Jude's hands on his shoulders, he opened his eyes to see him standing in front of him, straddling Delia's body. Right before his eyes was Jude's heavily swollen cock just begging for relief so he opened his mouth and Jude slid inside. Now he had his own cock deep inside Delia and Jude's cock deep inside his mouth. Maybe *this* was Jobin's paradise.

Toryn was afraid it was going to be awkward, not emotionally awkward but physically awkward but that was not the case at all. His whole body took the cadence of pleasuring both lovers at the same time. Each time he thrust his cock into Delia, he was able to swallow Jude's generous erection. Each pull-out stroke let him draw back his mouth as well. It took him quite a few strokes to get the rhythm of the mouth and the cock but it was exhilarating to feel the two massive cocks at work, one inside Delia and the other in his mouth. It was hard to decide where to place his focus as all his senses were being bombarded at once.

Delia's moans were delightful as he dug into her. He loved the wet slap as their bodies met, her legs cradling him and guiding him deep into her body. He relished Jude's cries as he took him deep into his mouth, sucking in his cheeks to force more pressure around the massive organ. He loved how the two cocks mimicked each other. As he slid into Delia's welcoming body, Jude moved his cock into Toryn's mouth, Delia's hot channel grasping him and his mouth grasping Jude's cock. He couldn't get enough of the feel of her warm, inviting body so soft and yet so strong and powerful as she gripped him. The contrast between her softness and the hardness of Jude's body was marked. He felt her soft lips with every stroke but Jude's hard flesh filled his mouth. He filled and was filled.

He felt the subtle changes and knew that Jude was getting close to going over the edge. Toryn knew how many times Jude had climaxed already but it didn't seem to matter. His captain threw back his head and howled like a wild animal as he came in Toryn's mouth, streams of hot liquid gushing down his throat. As his orgasm faded, Jude stepped away and collapsed on the bed, allowing Toryn to quicken the pace of his thrusts. It was as if the fluid from Jude had somehow increased the intensity of the lovemaking, invigorating him, forcing him to thrust harder into her. Suddenly he was so frantic that he was afraid he might be hurting her but he couldn't slow down and he sure as hell couldn't stop. Forcing himself to focus away from the all-consuming carnal delight for an instant, Toryn looked down at Delia's face. He needn't have worried for her eyes were on him, hazy with passion.

"I want all of you," she said softly and as he watched she put her hands to her breasts and began to play with her nipples. They were already tight as *eschens* so as soon as she touched them they lengthened. Just watching her nipples harden and lengthen seemed to have the same effect on Toryn's staff. Every tug, every nip made Toryn's erection burrow deeper and deeper inside her as if his cock was somehow attached to those sumptuous breasts. As she pulled and squeezed them, Toryn could feel her cunt getting softer, juicier, ready for the culmination of their pleasure.

Jude watched, mesmerized as Toryn hammered into Delia, her enjoyment of those gorgeous breasts tormenting Toryn as he reached higher and higher. He stared as she snaked one hand down her belly, making him wonder what kind of torture she had in store for Toryn now. He had to smile as she put out her long middle finger and bumped it against Toryn's cock as he rammed into her. As that naughty finger started to curl toward her clit, Jude crawled down the bed and sat cross-legged beside Delia, eager to view every minute of their pleasure. That finger tucked itself up under her hood and started to press and circle and Delia started to pant in her eagerness to reach fulfillment. Shoving her hand out of the way, Jude put his mouth to her clitoris and licked the little bud. He knew that wasn't enough, not nearly enough so, putting one leg over Delia's torso, he went on his hands and knees over her body, his mouth hovering above her clit and his solid cock hovering above her eager mouth. All he had to do was bend forward and that luscious little love bud popped into his eagerly awaiting mouth. He felt Delia's hand grab his cock and guide it to her mouth where she licked only the tip. Jude discovered he could suck her clit into his mouth from this angle and torment her while he felt Toryn pull back and wait, his cock poised just inside her. Delia's head lifted off the bed as she moved it up and down his cock, taking him deep into her mouth.

No one knew who went off first.

It might have been Delia with the triple torment of Toryn's cock as he began to press inside her plus Jude's voracious mouth devouring her clit and his rock-hard dick filling her mouth. Perhaps it was the perfect combination of all three.

Maybe it was Toryn, inside the tight, wet canal of a woman for the first time, pushing in as far as their close positions would allow.

Possibly it was Jude, his lips and tongue performing magic on Delia's clit while she returned the pleasure with her greedy mouth.

No one knew who triggered the chain reaction but it didn't really matter. The next thing Delia knew she was spasming with Jude's mouth right on her quivering clit at the same time as he exploded and shot his cream far down her throat. She could feel Toryn detonating inside her, filling her with his rich cum. Then everything went bright red behind her eyelids, then jet black as she fought to catch her breath.

Toryn felt her inner muscles quiver then clutch him tighter and tighter until she grabbed him like a fist and he knew she was up and over. That was it for him. Calling her name, he pumped madly into her. On and on he spewed his precious fluid as if there was no end to it.

Jude felt Delia's little clit stand to attention and knew that she was so close then his own body reached the point of no return and he flew off, bright lights behind his eyelids, his breath coming in labored pants.

Jude was the first to return to his body, his senses still fuzzy from the intense lovemaking. Drawing his leg back over

Delia's body, he fell on the bed beside her, eager to take her in his arms.

As soon as Toryn saw Jude move to the side, he allowed himself to collapse on top of Delia, capturing her with his body, unwilling to let her go. He felt his spent cock slowly slither from her body, his penis as exhausted as he was.

Delia watched Jude extricate himself from the tangle of their bodies then welcomed Toryn as he flopped on top of her, his generous erection quietly sliding from her body. No one spoke. No one moved.

Delia wondered what thoughts were going through Toryn's mind. Had he enjoyed making love with a woman? Judging by the volume of his cries at detonation, he liked it—a lot. Reaching down, she gently passed her hand down his silky hair, petting him, reassuring him.

Toryn rolled to his side, keeping his head in the crook of her arm, his leg bent across her body, unwilling to break the connection. Making love with another man was often loud and hard. Sometimes he and Jude lay spooned together afterwards but Jude's body was powerful and hard, his arms strong and muscular as they cradled him. Despite her profession this woman was still a woman. She had a woman's softness, a woman's touch and he found that was something he really liked, something he could come to crave. He loved having sex with Jude but a relationship between the three of them would fill a part of him that he hadn't even realized was missing. He could lie here forever with her hand gently stroking his hair, calming him, soothing him like you would a child. He felt Jude's leg tangle with his across her body and realized that he was cradling her from the other side. He felt an incredible peace and contentment being with these two people.

The lovers dozed off, exhausted by the arduous lovemaking. Delia woke first but lay quietly, wanting to forever etch this moment in her memory. How often did a woman get to make love with two of the greatest warriors in the galaxy? Not often enough. Delia was sure that was about to change, judging by the size of the twin erections growing alongside her body. She felt Jude shift first as he angled his body to nibble at her breast then Toryn moved to torment the mate with his mouth. It was such an odd feeling. Both her breasts were being teased at the same time and when she thought about that happening because two men were making love to her in concert, she felt her whole body ripen in anticipation. Being made love to by these two powerful men was indescribable.

On one side of her body, Jude was flicking her tight, little nipple with his tongue, never taking it into his mouth or biting hard enough to suit her. On the other side, Toryn took her bud in his mouth and pressed it down with his tongue then released it and sucked so hard it made her toes curl. Jude abandoned the torture with his tongue and took her little tip between his teeth and worried at it like a naughty terrier. Delia's torso tried to lift off the bed as he gently bit down then pulled with his teeth but she was imprisoned by the rock-hard bodies of her two lovers. It was hard to concentrate on what Jude was doing for Toryn had begun to nip sideways down her torso from her underarm to the top of her leg. Of course each nip needed to be soothed with a brushstroke of his tongue so how could she center on Jude's mouth with Toryn nipping and soothing her? Then Jude started a path of tiny bites down the other side of her torso and she didn't know where to focus. Oh dear Panton! What was she going to do when they made their journey down her body and both warriors arrived at that most aching of places between her legs? Uh-oh! Time to find out!

Toryn climbed off the bed and went to his knees at her feet, pulling her legs apart and holding one foot up by the heel. He lifted that foot to his eagerly awaiting mouth and proceeded to lick that most sensuous part of her body. Delia had walked on those feet her entire life, never imagining how very, very sensitive they were. Each swipe of his tongue made her nerve endings tingle and her body writhe. It was like someone was tickling her foot but the feeling was almost too erotic to be borne. He even managed to grab the tight skin with his teeth and nip her sole. Lowering her foot a bit, he separated her toes one by one and licked in between with his strong, very flexible tongue.

As she groaned, he raised his head to watch her writhing to the double torture of his tongue licking her foot and Jude nipping his way down her torso. He watched as Jude slid off the bed to kneel between her splayed legs. He could see the cream oozing from her, could imagine that he could even smell the rich, juicy liquid. He knew what Jude was going to do and could almost taste it himself before Jude even put his mouth to her. Setting his tongue to the bottom of her foot, he felt the shudder traverse her body as his male lover licked her creamy slit. Placing her foot on the floor, he looked on as Jude tucked his tongue right up into her vagina and sipped her juice.

She couldn't keep her upper body still as Jude was relentless in his devouring of her cunt. Toryn watched him seize her stiff little clit with his front teeth and tug it gently. He watched as a tiny tear slid down the side of her face. It was almost too much for her but Jude didn't seem to care as he continued his unrelenting pursuit of her orgasm. As Jude kept tugging her clit then poking it with the point of his tongue, Toryn moved forward and, putting his hand palm up, stuck his long middle finger inside her. He was delighted to feel her muscles seize his finger and he could feel her inner walls pulse with each tug of Jude's tongue on her clit. With his hand placed palm up under Jude's head, he was literally able to cup Jude's chin in his hand, letting him feel every movement of Jude's mouth and tongue as he pleasured Delia.

He knew the exact moment that her orgasm began. With his finger right inside her he felt the fluttering of her walls, then she bathed his finger in her rich juices just before she shot off. Her orgasm grabbed his finger and he knew the juices flowing down his finger were finding their way into Jude's mouth as well. It was intense.

He had been so busy with Delia's pleasure that his own pounding erection had gone unnoticed. Reaching up onto the bed, he grabbed the tube of lube and spread it on his aching cock. That taken care of, he went to his knees behind Jude and pulled him back toward his lap. Delia lay on the bed, unable to move and hoping that eventually her mind would be able to put together at least one coherent thought. But not right now.

Chapter Nine

ꕥ

Toryn could feel Jude shake as he realized what was in store for him. Putting one foot on each side of Toryn's legs, Jude's powerful legs held him suspended above Toryn's mighty cock as he waited for him to slide it home. He wasn't disappointed. Grabbing his massive hard-on in one steely fist, Toryn put his other arm around Jude and guided him down just enough to delicately circle his little puckered orifice with his giant tool. He could feel Jude's legs shivering, a combination of the effort needed to hold that powerful body above Toryn's cock and the sheer anticipation of that rod sliding home. Toryn decided to take pity on Jude and put him out of his misery so he pulled him down, that solid iron rod disappearing into the circle of drawn flesh.

At Jude's cry of anguish, Delia shot onto her elbows to see what was wrong. Her eyes grew wide as she watched the spectacle unfolding before her. From her vantage point on the bed, she was able to see Toryn's enormous erection disappear, bit by painful bit, into Jude's quivering body. She had known these men were strong and powerful but to watch Jude hold his body up and let it descend so slowly took great power and strength. Jude's upper body was drawn tight as a bow with the force of his slow descent and Toryn's upper body reflected the same tightness but from the sheer pleasure of Jude's body taking his cock. Toryn gripped his lover around the waist and began to guide him up and down his enormous shaft. Delia couldn't look away from this massive show of male strength and beauty.

Then Jude slowly rose to his feet, leaving Toryn's gorgeous cock standing at attention below him. Delia didn't understand why he would leave before completion then she watched as he turned to face Toryn and Toryn smiled at him as he sank down facing his lover, looking in his eyes as he took him inside his body. Now she understood. Jude leaned forward, hands on Toryn's shoulders, pressing a hard kiss on his mouth, forcing him to open his mouth and accept Jude's tongue inside. The two men groaned as their tongues dueled and Jude traced along the inside of Toryn's cheek with his sharp tongue. Now it was Jude who controlled the loveplay, taking his tongue from Toryn's mouth and rising up 'til that mighty cock of Toryn's almost drew out of him then dropping back down to take it far into his body. Delia reveled in the dynamic interplay of these two male beasts as they made love before her, their huge bodies straining, shiny with sweat as they rode to passion together. Suddenly she sat up and went to the floor with her glorious lovers. Taking a spot beside the two, she was able to lean in between them and take Jude's stiff cock in her mouth. Toryn looked on in delight as Delia joined them, helping pleasure Jude. Jude loved it. He took Toryn's massive cock inside him as Delia took his cock into her mouth.

Jude took hold of her head with his hands and pushed her down deep on his cock, forcing her to swallow all of him to the back of her throat while he sat with Toryn's solid weapon buried inside him. He gently drew her head up and down his cock, suspecting that she could smell the pleasure oozing from him. Toryn could feel her silky hair tickling his thighs, a marked contrast to the solid flesh pounding into Jude. He felt his need rise higher and higher until he shot into Jude, an endless stream.

Jude felt Toryn's release and relished the unending spasms of his lover's body. His head was reeling with more pictures of how the three of them could make love. Gently pulling Delia's head up so she wouldn't make him come, he said, "Go lie on the bed again and open your legs." At this stage, he could have asked her to sprout wings and fly and she would have tried to do it for him. She struggled to her feet and lay on the bed as before then he spoke to his navigator as he slowly stood and released Toryn's cock from the prison of his body.

"I want you to go down on her again," he said with a sly smile. Toryn was more than happy to comply and went to work on her delicious cunt while Jude looked on. Delia watched as this time it was Jude who grabbed the tube of lubricant, smoothing it liberally over his cock. She watched as his hand stayed on his erection as he stared at Toryn hungrily gobbling her up. She watched as he went behind Toryn and grabbed his hips to hold him still as he shoved past his navigator's tiny ring of flesh. Toryn's tongue lashed out at her in a frenzy as Jude's cock disappeared into his ass. Jude's hips shoved deep, forcing his cock far into Toryn's butt then drew out only to jam forward again. Delia could see why Toryn had enjoyed making love with her. It had been much softer. This was hard and solid. A good pounding into him while he sought her hole with his eager tongue.

Delia hated the thought of Toryn's gorgeous hard-on standing rampant but unused between his legs but alas there was no one to take it into their mouth or into their body. She could feel Jude pounding into Toryn from behind and knew he couldn't last much longer. All through their lovemaking it had been Toryn who had taken Jude and she had wondered if that was how they usually made love. Judging by what was happening now it was obvious that they took turns being the rear admiral. She had never made love with a rear admiral before as there were few of them in the fleet and here she was now making love with two of them.

Toryn began to howl and she knew it was all over for him. His body spasmed as Jude continued to ram his cock home then with a great shout Jude pumped furiously into his friend, trying to prolong the incredible pleasure but to no avail. He soared off into free fall, gushing into his lover's hole. With a sigh, Jude fell forward onto Toryn's back as Toryn laid his head on Delia's thigh.

Raising his head, Jude said to Delia, "That wasn't very fair."

"What do you mean?" she asked.

"We both came but you didn't get off."

"Not yet," she said with a coy little smile. Jude watched as she gently moved Toryn's head and got to her feet. Padding across the floor, she disappeared into the bathroom, leaving the two lovers entangled by the side of the bed. Toryn tried to relax as Jude pulled free then collapsed beside Toryn, his back against the bed. Toryn let his body fall to the floor and lay there unmoving, his crossed arms cradling his head. Finally summoning enough energy to roll to his side, he propped his head on his hand and gave Jude a slow perusal.

"I've got to say that you certainly have the look of a man who was well loved," he said with a wry laugh. "That woman is incredible. I didn't know what she would think about making love with both of us but I have to say that she sure seemed to embrace it with gusto."

"Gusto!" hooted Jude. "If she'd had any more gusto, I'd be just a hollow shell, a pale shadow of my former self." The two men sat in silence for a minute.

"What did it feel like making love with a woman for the first time?" Jude asked curiously. He couldn't remember his first time with a woman but he certainly remembered his first time with Toryn.

"I hear you're looking for a new navigator," the voice said at his back. Jude didn't even bother to turn around.

When the bartender finally turned one of his heads his way, Jude motioned to his drink and called, "I'll have the same."

"I said, I hear you're looking for a new navigator," the voice spoke again from behind him. The bartender arrived with Jude's drink then extended his rubbery appendage so Jude could pay for his drink by placing his thumb on the tiny screen embedded in the bartender's "hand" between his double claw and finger then sat to enjoy the fiery liquid.

"So I guess the great Jude Roland, bounty hunter extraordinaire, is starting to go deaf as well as get careless. That's how you lost your last navigator, isn't it?" said the same voice. As Jude slowly swiveled around, the crowd filling the other barstools scattered. Even the two-headed bartender stepped back. Jude's temper was legendary and so was his knife.

"You'd better hope you've recently said goodbye to the people you love," he said as he turned. He didn't even bother to take out the knife. He knew he'd have this son of a bitch's throat slit and be back to sipping his drink before the body even hit the floor. Preparing to face this arrogant asshole who was about to breathe his last, Jude swung around and the breath literally froze in his throat. The man behind him looked like a god, tall and muscular with eyes the color of the sea on Old Earth. His body armor hugged a wide torso and powerful arms but as Jude's eyes raked down his body, it was the huge bulge between his legs that drew Jude's total attention. Even as he stared, the bulge grew bigger and he could just imagine that generous cock rearing up as this man covered him and slid in from behind.

He'd never in his entire life thought about having sex with another man. By Panton, he was known across the galaxy as the consummate ladies' man but that was all forgotten as he was consumed by lust for this stranger. So not only did he take him on as navigator, an hour later they were in the captain's cabin and his new navigator was greasing Jude's hole and revealing what was in the bulge of his flight suit. For the first time in his adult life, when Jude saw the size of that tremendous erection, he felt unsure. He could find any scumbag in the galaxy and bring him in. He could navigate through any star system without a map. He could kill a man with his bare hands but taking that cock into his body looked impossible, impossible and very painful. He was surprised how gentle this powerful man was with him and how careful he was as he pressed his cock into Jude's virgin ass. And they had been lovers off and on ever since. Jude couldn't wish for a better man at his back, in all situations.

Toryn's voice drew him back to the present.

"Where were you?" Toryn asked with a laugh. He'd watched the various emotions shifting across Jude's face and wondered what was going through his head. Jude looked down at Toryn, a smile of contentment on his face.

"I was remembering the first time we met," he admitted.

"You didn't really make a very good first impression," Toryn snorted. "But I was more than willing to forgive you once I eased my cock into your tight little hole." Jude shivered at Toryn's words, at the remembrance of that huge cock almost stretching him past the limits of his endurance.

"She fills a part of me that I didn't know was missing," Toryn quietly said.

"I know what you mean. I felt the same way the first time we made love," Jude said.

"Hey there." They looked up to see Delia standing in the doorway of the bathroom. It was obvious from the look on her face that she had heard their conversation. "You know, I've never made love with a rear admiral before. This time I got to make love with two rear admirals," she said, trying to keep a straight face. Toryn looked at Jude, Jude looked at Toryn and with a burst of energy they scrambled to their feet and, laughing, took off after her. Delia yelped and ran into the bathroom, the two lovers hot on her heels.

Jude was the first to reach her and he swept her up into his arms, letting her put her arms around his neck. Turning circles with her, the bathroom was filled with her laughter.

"Put me down," she cried. That's what she said but that was the farthest thing from her mind. She never wanted him to put her down. She wanted to stay with these two men forever.

"Hold her for a minute, will ya?" he said as he handed her to Toryn. She loved the feel of Jude's body but Toryn's was just as strong and powerful, the muscles in his arms and chest bunching and rippling beneath the skin as he took her and held her close. Delia just held her breath and reveled in the feel of Toryn's warm skin against hers.

"Ready!" Jude called. They looked around to see water coming from various showerheads and low-level hidey-holes in the shower chamber. Delia had the distinct feeling that she was finally going to find out about Number Two and Number Five.

Lying on the bed later with Jude between her and Toryn, Delia mused about the delights of Number Two and Number Five. These warriors were very inventive in the shower. They were probably going to have to refill the soap dispenser after this last adventure. They had even introduced her to Number Eight, an introduction that went with some positions that she didn't think should have been possible. Correction, positions that could only be possible with three.

Lying with her head on Jude's chest, she ran her fingers over the taut skin of his belly. For such a hard man, he could be a very gentle lover but as she had seen his lovemaking with Toryn, he could be demanding and fierce in his passion as well. As she explored, her hand bumped Toryn's, which was making its own foray across the same smooth skin. When their fingers touched, Toryn reached to link his fingers with hers and together they ran their joined hands over Jude's washboard stomach. Toryn dragged her hand with his down, down Jude's belly until they were on top of his cock.

When Jude felt the hands come to rest on his penis, he pushed himself back so he was leaning on the pillows propped up against the wall. He didn't want to miss a second of this! It was a bit awkward but Toryn and Delia ran their linked hands up and down Jude's shaft with the anticipated result. His beautiful cock got longer and longer until Toryn leaned forward and took it into his mouth.

Delia watched his cheeks become hollow as he used the pressure to suck that powerful tool of delight. Not wanting to be left out, Delia clambered over Jude's body and, lying with her head touching his side, took Toryn's unattended cock into her mouth. Jude moaned, Toryn groaned, Delia smiled. Delia tried to imitate what she had seen Toryn doing to Jude's erection and she must have gotten it right for Toryn used his hips to shove his penis deeper into her mouth. He was so big it was difficult to take all of him at once but she tried. She didn't have much choice the way he pressed himself far into her mouth.

She felt Jude roll away so she lifted her head to see what he was up to. He had the lube. Looking down at Toryn, she saw him smile as he watched Jude coat his massive cock with it. Gently pulling away from Delia, Toryn waited 'til Jude was done then he turned his back to him and, putting his legs outside Jude's, impaled himself on Jude's very swollen cock as Jude held it steady for him. Delia shifted a tiny bit so her head was right on Jude's chest and she was able to watch close-up. She was always amazed that such a massive weapon could disappear so easily into such a small opening. Jude howled as his cock made its way into Toryn's ass. Toryn yelled as his ass opened to receive the great tool. And Delia got to watch.

"Get the lube," Toryn asked between clenched teeth. Reaching across Jude, she grabbed the tube, not understanding what he was going to do. "Put it on me," he said. Unscrewing the lid, she squirted some across her fingers then used her soft hand to coat him. "Put the rest on you," he growled. Now she understood. Now she started to shake. Reaching between her legs, she spread her honeyed lips with the lube. "You know what I want," Toryn whispered to her. Turning her back to him, she crouched between his legs and let her self down, down, down until she reached his cock and it disappeared up, up, up inside her. "Next time I'm going to put that great big cock inside your little butthole," he said into her ear. "Would you like that?" She nodded shakily, remembering the feelings she shared as she watched them in the shower. All that cock going into her little puckered hole! That was enough to set her body aquiver and Toryn knew it.

Jude couldn't believe what was happening. Toryn was mounted on his cock but Toryn in turn had Delia impaled on his. Toryn put his hands back behind him on the bed and Delia put her hands on Toryn's legs.

All Delia could think of was how strong these men were to be able to make love like this. It was a bit awkward to get the rhythm of three but soon she was riding up and down on Toryn's cock as he rode up and down on Jude's. This time she knew she was the one to blow first, going off with a harsh keening cry.

Toryn felt her grab him tightly and he followed quickly behind. Delia lifted her body off Toryn and let him increase the rhythm with Jude, slamming down as Jude pounded into him. Jude's body shook as he poured into his lover, the white cream running from Toryn's body. Toryn collapsed back onto Jude's chest then slid to the side, resting his leg over Jude's body. Delia crawled along the foot of the bed and spooned Toryn from behind.

"I loved that," she said to them. "That was so intense. I'm glad our screens are in place. I don't think my heart could take it otherwise."

"Your heart? I don't think my cock could take it," Jude said.

"I love making love with Jude," Toryn said, "but I love making love with you as well. You bring a softer, gentler side to our lovemaking and I like that."

"What just happened didn't seem very soft and gentle to me," Delia said with a laugh. She ran her hand down his arm and laced her fingers with his.

"You know what I mean," he said, a serious tone in his voice.

"Yes, I do," Delia said.

Jude, who had been listening to their conversation, said, "Delia, we want you to stay with us."

"Stay with you. You mean like a live-in mistress?" she asked, appalled that they might even consider that.

Toryn and Jude both laughed. "No, as a bounty hunter."

"Me, a bounty hunter. What makes you think I could be a bounty hunter?" she asked, interest evident in her voice.

"You would be perfect," Toryn said. "You are beautiful and feminine yet you're the best fighter pilot in the Wardelian League."

"You look fragile yet you could kick anybody's butt in a fight," Jude added. "No one would ever suspect you were a bounty hunter until it was too late, plus the truth is that we don't want to let you go. We want you to stay with us and be our lover."

"I would love to stay but I do have my own navigator and I definitely can't go anywhere without her."

"She can join us. If she's your navigator we know she'd have to be good, almost as good as me," Toryn said with a smirk. Delia leaned forward and bit him on the shoulder.

"Ouch," he said as Delia licked the little red mark.

"I need to see what she says but I think she's ready for a change, same as I am, but I suspect she'll be signing on strictly as a navigator."

"Why don't we just wait and see," Jude said. "Why don't we just wait and see."

"That sounds great to me but now we need to go back to the cowboy planet and pick up my navigator or at least talk to her." It was at that precise moment that the cabin door slid open and a very angry woman stalked in. She stood just inside the door and took in the scene on the bed.

"Here I am searching all over the galaxy for you and I find you safely tucked in bed with not just one but two stud muffins. You disappear off the face of the planet with no word to me and I find you in bed with these two, two…pieces of eye candy," she said, sputtering as she gestured at Toryn and Jude. Delia knew Lina had been reading those Old Earth romance novels again. Jude and Toryn burst out laughing. They didn't know what a stud muffin was or eye candy for that matter but they could tell by the tone of her voice that it might not be a compliment. Lina stalked over to the bed. "So you think this is funny, do you? I've been frantic with worry and here she is safe and sound having sex with you two."

Jude was the first to respond. Moving to the side of the bed, he rose to his feet towering over Lina. "None of this is Delia's fault. I kidnapped her to exchange her for Toryn, my navigator—"

"That would be me," Toryn said.

"Who had been captured by Brachan." Lina's face paled at the mention of Brachan.

"You were going to turn her over to Brachan," she hissed.

"I did turn her over to Brachan," he admitted. Delia came around the bed and stood beside Jude.

"He did turn me over to Brachan but not without a brilliant plan that saved his navigator and me. And we weren't having sex either, we were making love," she said, her hands on her hips. Toryn coughed into his hand at the mention of what he considered to be Jude's less-than-brilliant plan.

Lina threw herself at Delia. "I was so worried. I thought I wasn't going to see you again." Toryn got off the bed and came to stand with Delia and Jude. Lina stepped back and looked at the three of them. "You do realize that you're all naked," she said with a laugh.

"Trust me. For what we were doing we needed to be naked," Delia assured her.

"You mean that you were making love with both these men…at the same time?"

"That's exactly what I mean," she said happily. Lina looked at Delia, really looked at her glowing face then she looked at Jude and Toryn.

Can I try too?" she asked.

"Guess we found our other bounty hunter," Jude said to Toryn but Toryn wasn't listening. He was much too busy staring at *The Renegade*'s new co-navigator.

The stories passed through the galaxy, from planet to planet, from star system to star system and for centuries to come people would always speak in hushed tones of the bounty hunters of *The Renegade*.

ABSOLUTE TRUST

&

Dedication

ꕥ

Thank you to my husband and sons for your wholehearted support in this crazy venture called writing. To Meghan, my amazing editor – you make me feel like I can do anything. J.B. – thanks for the right words for all craft airborne. Brynn, Bronwyn, Cindy and Dakota, thanks for your faith, encouragement and friendship. You're such dear friends.

Chapter One

In the year of Jobin 1276

ꟸ

Following Delia and Jude, Micah looked around the dark, crowded Chendan bar. He knew what he was seeing was only a façade, the people drinking and dancing, laughing and flirting. The real business of pleasure was taking place in rooms that you had to know about.

"Come on," Delia mouthed, as she swung round to make sure he was still behind them.

He moved forward reluctantly. Micah O'Brien had little use for these overcrowded dens of self-gratification. He'd had enough of places like this as a young cadet when he'd first joined the forces of the Wardelian League, but he hadn't said no to Delia and Jude when they'd asked him to join them. They were more than just fellow bounty hunters, they were also his friends. In his profession good friends were hard to come by and well worth keeping.

The Renegade was only docked on Chend long enough to give the crew a brief respite. The last trip to Jardalez had been trouble from the get-go and Jude Roland, the captain of the star cruiser, knew everyone needed some R&R.

"It's a good thing you decided to come with us," Jude said before they left the cruiser. "You know Delia won't take no for an answer."

So even though he'd rather be elsewhere, Micah wasn't.

He watched as Delia tried talking to Jude over the raucous music. Jude just shook his head to let her know her efforts at conversation were futile..She shrugged, then waved to someone across the cavernous room. Micah had to laugh as she grabbed Jude's hand and began to make a path through the tempestuous storm of bodies on the dance floor, pulling him along in her wake.

She is definitely a force to be reckoned with. Like all the female bounty hunters of The Renegade, he thought.

They were like a secret weapon with their beauty and grace. Many a quarry had underestimated them and ended up on the ground in handcuffs before they knew what hit them. These women were strong and fierce, their natural abilities augmented by sensor implants, their innate fierceness made stronger by their loyalty to their fellow hunters.

Micah loved women, but the women who were part of the bounty hunters of *The Renegade* drew him in another way. He admired their courage and their loyalty, but most of all he envied the trust he saw between them and their partners. Delia and Jude were hunters together but also lovers and they shared that bond with Toryn, one of the ship's navigators. That was what Micah wanted—trust, in life and in love.

"Don't worry," Delia had said to him. "One of these days it'll happen. Probably when you least expect it."

He wanted trust and he also wanted Layla. But he knew he couldn't have her. She was one of the youngest hunters on the star cruiser, while it seemed like a lifetime since he'd seen twenty-four. She was just too young.

Micah fought his way through the crowd, trying valiantly to ignore the naughty hands that reached out to rub his cock or fondle his butt as he attempted to keep up with Delia. She continued to drag Jude through the swarm of gyrating bodies, finally hauling him out on the other side of the dance floor, where they climbed a short staircase and headed for a booth against the wall. He wondered who she was smiling at as she slipped onto one bench seat while her partner squeezed his massive frame in opposite her.

He realized that he'd rather be in close combat with the enemy than try to navigate this sea of groping tentacles. For

Jobin's sake, he was thirty-six years old with a warrior's scarred body. Who would want to put their hands on his old carcass? Lots of people, if the number of gropes per step were any indication.

Feeling like he was being squeezed out of a *jergajumpa,* Micah pulled free of the mass to make his way to the table where Delia and Jude were ensconced. Taking in his exasperated expression, Delia motioned to the space opposite and yelled, "You've got that same look you get after you and Jude have been sparring. Why don't you sit down?"

He wanted to shake his head at the ways of Fate. Layla was there. He didn't need to see her to know. It was always that way when she was close by. He could tell by the rising of the hair on the back of his neck and the rising of his cock. It may have been dark in the bar, but he didn't need any light to know that she was sitting in the shadows beside Delia. He slid in next to Jude as the DJ slipped on a slow dance tune and the music turned from raucous to sultry.

"Micah, you know Layla," Delia said.

He certainly did. She'd been recruited by Jude after he'd pulled her off Staar, one of the Fangian bounty hunters. No one messed with the Fangians. That was one of those unspoken Galactic rules. They fought dirty and particularly liked it when the odds were against them. Hand-to-hand combat was their forte, with knives and short swords being their weapons of choice. None of that had mattered to Layla when Staar showed up drunk and thought he could enter the restricted area she was guarding on TLar2.

The story circulating aboard *The Renegade* was that he'd just been fooling around hoping somehow to impress her, but instead had landed flat on his back. He hadn't been too drunk to fight back, it just hadn't made any difference. Jude had recruited her on the spot. And Micah hadn't known a moment's peace since.

When Layla was around, he tried not to get too close and knew she thought he was rude because of it. But it had more to do with the perpetual hard-on she gave him, a hard-on that kept him edgy and unfulfilled. Like now.

Micah swallowed, not sure if he could speak. She leaned forward and his heart stepped up its beat as he took in her delicate face.

Giving him a quick smile, she spoke. "Hello, Micah."

Micah managed to blurt out a quick hello. He was pretty sure she had no idea how her presence affected him and he wanted to keep it that way.

It was Jude who broke the uneasiness of the moment. "Delia, Micah. What do you want to drink? I'll go grab them."

"I'm going to have one of those cute little girly drinks," Delia said. "You know what I mean Jude, one of those that come with the fruit and the tiny umbrella."

Jude held up his hands. "No way am I ordering that at the bar. You'll have to come with me."

Delia slid out of the seat and turned to Layla. "You want another drink?"

Layla covered her glass with her hand. "No. I'm fine."

"Micah?"

"I'll have a beer."

Jude pushed at Micah, forcing him to slide over and let him out. Micah watched as the two bounty hunters made their way to the bar, Delia playfully pinching Jude's ass as he sauntered in front of her.

He turned to see Layla laughing.

"They're so happy together. I like that," she explained.

"Very happy. Especially with Toryn, their other lover," Micah added.

"That must be wonderful. To have people like that in your life."

"What about you?" Micah questioned, not really wanting to hear the answer. "You have someone special?"

Layla looked away.

"What's wrong?" Micah asked.

"There is somebody. But I don't think he's interested."

Micah's body tensed as jealousy nipped at him. He didn't want to think of her with anyone else. "How could he not be interested?"

"What do you mean?"

"How could he not be interested? You're young and beautiful and a nasty little fighter."

"Thank you. I think," she said, looking into his eyes. "But he'd say he's too old for me, even though I know he has to hide behind a chair whenever I'm in the room. He thinks I don't notice that he's hard for me. Like right now."

Micah jumped as her foot gently landed on his cock. The little minx must have slipped off her shoe and was now giving his hard-on a massage.

"See what I mean?"

Micah wanted to push her away, but it felt too good. The heat of her body burning him through the supple leather of his breeches, the naughty flex of her toes down the length of his shaft, the insistent pressure on his eager flesh. *She's playing with fire and she knows it.*

"I'm too old for you. I've tasted too much nastiness in the galaxy. I'm not a nice man. You need to look for someone better, closer to your own age."

"Ah, you mean like Shayne."

Micah flinched.

"Or perhaps Roake?"

Micah frowned.

"How about Tayller? He's only a few years older than me. What about him?"

Micah didn't like this conversation at all. He knew he couldn't have her, but he didn't want to think of her with any of the other bounty hunters either.

Layla dragged her foot off Micah's erection, slipped her shoe on and stood.

"Where are you going?" he demanded.

"I'm going to see if one of those young bounty hunters would like to fuck me all night long." And she strode off into the crowd.

Micah took just enough time to use his communication implant to send a message to Jude, then took off after Layla. She'd made it across the dance floor before he managed to catch up and grab her arm. She tried to shake off his hand, but he pulled her along a corridor until he came to a door with a green light above it, indicating that the chamber was available.

Micah pulled his captive into the room, activating the locking mechanism with a flick of his hand as he slammed the door behind them. Pushing her onto the bed, he flipped the shoulder catches on his torso armor and threw it to the floor. His hands shook as he tore off his shirt and tossed it aside. Grabbing the nearest chair, he sat down, pulled off his boots and socks and shot to his feet again. His *classen*-hard cock sprang free the moment he yanked down his black leather breeches. They hit the floor and he advanced on her like a wild creature scenting its prey.

"Listen to me, sweetheart. If anybody fucks you all night long, it's going to be me."

* * * * *

From the determined look on his face, Layla knew it would be wise to be afraid, very afraid. *This is what happens when you tease a beast,* was the first thought that went through her head as Micah moved toward her. It was hard to catch her breath as she took in the sight of his powerful body, the scars of battle across his chest, his arms and legs roped with heavy muscle. Except one look at his arousal sent all fear flying. She wanted that inside her, filling her.

But after the way he'd made her wait, she was going to make him work for it. Before he reached the bed, she turned and attempted to crawl away.

He just laughed and grabbed her ankle.

"No way, darling. No way are you getting away from me."

Layla struggled, rolling to her back so she could kick out at him with her other foot. But he was too fast. Now he had her by both ankles.

"I'm not Staar. You won't catch me off guard like you did him," he said with a wicked smile.

She tried to flick her legs and force him to release her, but it was futile. He was too strong.

"I'm not letting you go. You think those young men can please you. They don't know the first thing about pleasing a woman like you."

"So what are you gonna do, old man?" she teased. *Maybe teasing's not a good idea when the man has fucking on his mind.*

He gave her his answer as he crept up her body. "I already told you what I'm gonna do. I'm gonna fuck you all night long. Someone needs to show you what happens to little girls who like to tease."

Layla sighed into his mouth as he licked a thin line across her top lip. *Resistance is futile. I want him too much.* Reaching up, she ran her fingers through his long silky hair, letting the cool locks caress her skin. He responded by nibbling at her bottom lip.

Drawing back, he growled. "You taste so young and so sweet. I wonder if the rest of you tastes as sweet. I guess I'll just have to find out." Bracketing her legs with his, he went to his knees and pulled her to a sitting position. She let him flick the shoulder catches on her torso armor and pull it away from her body, leaving her in a long-sleeved black T-shirt. Throwing the armor to the side, he lowered her to the bed again and, still kneeling, gently sat back on her.

She couldn't take her eyes off his cock. She wished she were nude so that when he leaned over her belly, the soft flesh of his erection would rub against her. His shaft was long and thick and she knew the skin would be smooth and supple as it caressed her stomach.

"Are you naked under that shirt?" he asked.

"You'll just have to find that out as well," Layla said, saucy invitation in her voice.

He tugged the garment free of her black leather breeches.

"My pleasure," he said, locking his gaze with hers. She watched the hunter being replaced by the lover. Now that he had her where he wanted her, his ferocious need seemed to be tempered with something else—something more tender.

At the first touch of his rough hands as they burrowed under the hem of her shirt, her eyes drifted shut. *No, it will be our pleasure*, she thought.

Up his hands skimmed until they reached the lacy cups of her bra.

"Is it white?" he whispered.

She shook her head.

"Is it red?"

Same answer.

Her eyes flew open as he slid off the end of the bed. He grabbed her hand and, pulling her to her feet, threw her a mischievous smile.

"I guess I'll discover for myself."

Layla shivered as he grabbed the bottom of her shirt and tugged it over her head. It fell to the floor as he stepped back and looked down at her.

"Black. That's my very favorite color," he said as he ran one finger along the top of her breasts, letting it linger a moment in the valley between.

"I love how the black looks against your pale skin. Those little freckles above your left breast seem to be begging for my tongue."

He suited action to his words, licking her sensitive flesh.

"Those boys could never please you like I can. You know that, don't you?"

She whimpered.

"I'll take that as a yes."

Layla shivered as he gently undid the front closure and drew the lacy material away from her breasts. Taking the thin straps in his calloused hands, he slid them down, pushing her arms behind her back at the same time.

"Keep your hands there. Look how that thrusts your beautiful breasts to me."

He sat on the bed and pulled her to stand between his legs. She loved the way his hard cock bobbed as he moved.

"That's much better. Now it's so easy for me to put my mouth on you," Micah said.

Layla giggled as he nipped across her belly, as his tongue licked around her navel. But the laughter died in her throat as he found her nipple and took it in his mouth. *I want more. Give me more,* she silently begged.

And he did.

She had to clasp her hands behind her back to keep them from finding their way to him, to draw his head closer. She loved how he knew just what pleased her, what she wanted as his clever tongue flicked the tight nub, as his lips kissed a teasing path to her other breast. She moaned and he paused and raised his head.

"Would those boys make you feel like that?"

Forgetting his command to keep her hands clasped, she reached out and cupped his face. "Shut up about those boys. I never wanted them to touch me, only you. I only want your hands on me, your mouth on me, your cock in me."

He grinned. "I'm so very glad to hear that."

"Enough talk," Layla said.

Stepping back, she grabbed a chair and sat down. "Take off my boots for me," she ordered.

Rising to his full six foot three inches, Micah came and stood before her. "I'd be delighted," he said. Kneeling, he took one foot and began to undo her bootlaces.

"I think I really like having you supplicatory at my feet."

Micah laughed and swooped up to give her a quick kiss on the lips. Tugging off one of her boots, he got rid of her sock and started to work on the other boot. While he was busy with her lace, Layla bent her leg and gently rubbed his cock with her foot.

"That's a busy little foot you have," he said, seizing it so he could bring it to his mouth and lick the sensitive sole.

She couldn't believe how easily he was able to turn the tables on her. But she loved this game of give and take.

He made quick work of her other boot and sock, then got to his feet, pulling her up with him. Before she could protest, he took over the chair.

"Take off those lovely leather breeches for me. I want to see what you're wearing underneath."

She gave him a naughty smile. He returned it.

"Ah, maybe you're not wearing anything underneath. Why don't you show me?"

Layla was going to take full advantage of this opportunity to tease him. Clasping her hands in front, she raised her arms over her head and stretched. The little maneuver had the desired effect. She saw his quick intake of breath and the clenching of the muscles in his belly.

As she slowly lowered her hands, he reached out for her. She slapped them away.

"My show. You watch," she said, chastising him.

He laughed.

Popping the snap at the waist, she grabbed the tab and pulled down the zipper bit by bit.

"Wait," Micah cried, as she put her thumbs at the waistband ready to haul them down and off.

She looked askance at him. *For Jobin's sake, don't let him have changed his mind.*

"Turn around and bend over. I want to see how the leather cradles your gorgeous ass."

Layla was more than happy to oblige. Anything to make him squirm. Giving him her back, she made a sort of exaggerated bow, allowing the supple material to be drawn nice and tight across her butt. Straightening slightly, she put her hands at the waistband of the pants and drew them down, making sure she took her time sliding them over the curve of her behind. She shimmied them down her legs and off.

His moan told her he was enjoying the view of the thin strip of material bisecting her cheeks.

"Oh shit, I'm not sure my old heart can take this."

Layla swung back to him, eager to keep pushing. Her tone was low, silky. "Do you think you could undo the bows for me, the little red ones at the side?"

She was sure there was a definite quiver in his hands as he reached out and tugged at the tiny strings.

"Open your legs just a bit," he said.

It was almost enough to make her swoon as he took hold of the delicate fabric and pulled. As he dragged it from her, he used an upward motion so the silky material rubbed her clit. Micah knew her body so well, knew exactly what made her body hum.

Boldly Layla moved to him and straddled his legs. Taking his hard-on in hand, she sank down, seating him fully. Something shifted within her. It was as if the room were spinning for an instant as she sat with his cock imbedded in her. Somehow his thoughts rippled through her very essence, telling her what he liked, what he wanted to do to her. Nothing like this had ever happened before.

"That feels so good having you tight around my cock," he said.

Layla used her inner muscles to squeeze then release.

"And that feels even better," Micah pronounced.

Putting her hands on his shoulders, she leaned forward and rocked gently on his erection.

"And how about that?" she asked as she swayed over him.

He gave her a wicked smile as his reply, a wicked smile accompanied by the sliding of his hands under her legs.

She should have known that he would wrest control from her, but as soon as he lifted her and let her slide back down on his erection, she didn't really care. He wanted what she wanted.

Micah made it look effortless. She could see the muscles in his upper arm flexing each time he raised her up. It was amazing how he could hold her suspended with only the head of his cock inside her. Then he'd let her descend. He teased her, shifting the rhythm. Sometimes he'd make it slow and languorous until she wanted to tell him to hurry up. Then he'd make it fast and forceful, slapping up into her with each downstroke. It was like a hurricane building inside her, swirling more and more rapidly, carrying both of them in its path.

She bit his shoulder as the storm broke, his last strokes frantic as he fought to stay with her.

* * * * *

The soft whispers of her breath tickled Micah's neck as Layla lay against his chest. He was glad they were sitting as he knew he was too weak to move. With one hand, he drew idle circles on her back, feeling the light sheen her soft skin bore from their love-making. The other hand clutched possessively at her waist.

What in Jobin's name just happened? The minute I put my tongue on her smooth belly I could swear I knew exactly what she wanted me to do to her.

Layla sighed against him as he smoothed his fingers over her silken flesh.

I knew how hard it was for her to keep those hands behind her back when all she wanted to do was pull me closer. I knew she'd be so bold as to climb into my lap and take me inside her. I just can't figure out how I knew.

Layla stirred, pulling back and placing her hands on his chest. "I love having you inside me." She separated her fingers and ran them down his muscled chest. "It was amazing, like nothing I've ever felt before." She continued to lightly stroke his heated flesh. "What happened? There was some kind of link between us, wasn't there? Did you feel it?"

Micah nodded. "It was almost as if your voice were softly speaking through my veins. It was hardly a voice, really, more your thoughts caressing me, guiding me."

Layla grabbed his shoulders as he quickly got to his feet. "What's the matter? Where are you going?" She held on tightly to him as he crossed to the bed, moaned as he drew his penis from her and set her down on the silky sheets.

"I'm taking up where I left off. I told you I was going to fuck you all night long and, although I'm not young, the night is."

Layla laughed. "There didn't seem to be much wrong with your ability to perform, old man." She bent her legs and tried to push herself away as Micah tickled her for teasing him.

"Who you calling an old man?"

"You. You're way older than I am."

Micah grew serious. "But that doesn't matter to you, does it?"

She searched his face. "No it doesn't."

"Good, because I've got some things I'd like to show you." With that, he lifted her legs and set them over his shoulders.

"Micah? What are you doing?" she asked, curiosity in her voice.

"I'm just going to see how sweet you taste."

"But there?"

"No one has ever gone down on you? Those men you've been with before must have been lousy lovers," he said, shaking his head.

"Not lousy, just young. I guess being with an older man has its benefits. More experience and all," she said smiling up at him.

"And I'm about to show you one of those benefits,' he said with a devilish grin.

He loved her breathy sigh as he rubbed his rough cheek along the tender skin of her thigh, her throaty moan as he gently bit along the same path. He felt her trepidation as he gently flicked her labia with his tongue.

"Oh great Jobin, Micah. Do lovers really do this?" she whispered.

"I don't know about other lovers, but we're going to."

Micah slicked the flat of his tongue up her slit, parting her fleshy lips in the journey. She was so slippery and creamy for him that he could die from the sweet taste of her. Fingers of desire swept along his skin, but he sensed her desire as well as his own. She guided him to what she wanted to know, the feeling of his tongue probing inside her, gently at first then more forceful.

He tongued her entrance, smearing her essence over his lips, pressing past her tight opening. Her taste shimmered along his tongue, sweet and spicy like a vintage wine he'd once sampled on Tlai'dan. It was intoxicating, addicting, and he wanted more. His tongue speared her, mimicking what his cock would do when he slipped inside her. Her juice slipped down his chin, driving him to push harder, deeper.

He felt her hovering, flickering on the edge of orgasm. He heard the soft rustle in his mind as she told him to make her come, right away, but he wanted to watch her when she went over.

"No, no," she cried, trying to grab at him as he let her legs slip and got to his feet.

Hooking his arms under her thighs, he slid inside her and leaned forward over her body. "I'm going to let you see what you taste like, see just how sweet you are." He took her mouth in a slow kiss, slipping his tongue inside, spreading her essence over her own lips. His blood raced as she answered him by licking his mouth, lapping her juice from his chin. It was too much.

It rippled through his mind that she was ready to be fucked. *Good.* For there was no gentle preamble, no soft words or tender gestures. Gripping her tightly he slammed into her, pulling her toward him with each stroke. The slap of flesh on flesh, her cries of hunger, his moans of urgency, the tangle of words as they flashed into fulfillment together.

Micah slowly collapsed on top of Layla, his cock still within her. Rolling to his back, he took her with him, so she lay sprawled along the length of his body. His eyes drifted shut as he tried to make sense of what had happened. On the one hand, it had seemed so primitive, so much like a claiming, but on the other hand it had felt so right, like coming home.

His eyes flew open at the sharp poke of her chin to his sternum.

"So you think you can keep this up all night, sailor?" she teased.

He flexed his cock inside her. "Oh, most definitely, little girl."

* * * * *

Normally he wouldn't have been pulling security detail on *The Renegade,* but it was their first stopover in more than a month and, being the "old man" of the crew, Micah had volunteered to stay behind. He didn't think he was that old, but when the others had said they were off to a night of carousing on Ratuja, he realized that he just wasn't interested.

He kept thinking about Layla, but she would have gone off with the rest of the crew and who could blame her with the way he'd been avoiding her for the last three months?

As he scanned the rows of compuscreens, Micah could still see the look in her eyes when he'd said that it had been a mistake. She'd taken it stoically, but he couldn't help but feel that pushing her away had been the stupidest thing he'd ever done.

He couldn't tell her how he'd felt when they'd been making love. The connection had been too strong, stronger than anything he'd had with anyone else. She was his connection, his soul mate, but he still felt that he was too old for her, too old and much too acquainted with the darker side of life.

Now he just felt restless and unsettled.

Thank Jobin it was easy to maintain security on the ship. All he had to do was sit by the bank of compuscreens in the security bay and watch. That was how he became aware of what was happening in the captain's chamber.

He heard the sound of voices and used the remocontrol to swivel the camerata to see who was in the captain's quarters. The device revealed a naked Jude Roland reclining on his bed. Micah knew he shouldn't keep watching. He knew he should switch off the compuscreen. But he couldn't raise his hand to deactivate it.

He thought all the bounty hunters had gone ashore with the rest of the crew, but judging by what was going on in

Jude's cabin, it was obvious that some of them had decided to stay behind. He could see why!

Micah had gone to the academy with Jude Roland, had fought beside him for six or seven years in the forces, then joined him as a bounty hunter a few years ago. He'd seen his captain drunk. He'd seen the man wounded. He'd seen him angry. He'd seen him naked. But he'd never seen him naked and aroused. Micah couldn't take his eyes off that cock, so heavy that it bowed toward the captain's navel.

Jude was lying propped against a jumble of pillows and watching someone out of Micah's field of vision. He saw Jude take his enormous hard-on in hand and run his fist up and down it, gently at first. Then the captain spat in his hand and used the lubrication to up the rhythm as he gripped tighter, closing his eyes to the bliss. Someone must have called to him, for he languidly opened his eyes to look at the figure offscreen again.

Micah willed his hand to lift and flick the deactivation switch, but he found that he just couldn't. Then his hand reached out and he breathed a sigh of relief, but it was short-lived as it touched the remocontrol again.

Now Jude was smiling at someone and holding out his hand, inviting that person to join him on the bed. Micah gasped as Toryn came into view.

Praise Jobin!

Toryn's erection wasn't as long as the captain's, but it was thicker and so solid and heavy that it moved slowly with each step the navigator took.

The hunters of *The Renegade* were a tight group. They had to be when their very lives depended on the trust they had for each other. As long as everyone did their job he couldn't care less what went on in the privacy of somebody else's chamber. Or so he thought until now.

As Micah stared at the screen, Toryn climbed on the huge bed from the bottom and crawled toward Jude, his heavy sac swinging between his legs. From this angle, Micah could see Toryn's tight butt as he playfully made his way to the captain. Jude was laughing and talking to his navigator as he urged him forward, but his face changed the moment Toryn straddled his body as he crept forward.

Suddenly Micah could imagine what that cock of Toryn's would feel like as it gently touched Jude's in passing. The skin would be soft, but the shaft would be *classen* hard, the two massive rods nudging each other.

Micah's cock began to respond as he imagined that caress against his own shaft, a foreign feeling to have another man's body so close, so intimate, but he found himself drawn to the idea of that pleasure nonetheless.

He watched as Toryn set his hands on the bed on each side of Jude's powerful chest, allowing him to lean forward and take Jude's mouth with his own, then tracing it with his tongue before gently sliding inside. Micah's cock jumped as the men pleasured each other with mouth and tongue and then it throbbed as Toryn drew back and began to kiss a path down Jude's neck.

Micah closed his eyes, but the picture was even more vivid, etched in his brain. He opened his eyes languorously to see Toryn flicking one nipple with his tongue while squeezing the other between his thumb and forefinger. Jude lifted off the bed while pleasure raced through him. Micah rose up off the chair in time with Jude as he watched the scene unfold. His whole body clenched as Toryn backed up, licking down Jude's taut belly, Jude laughing as Toryn tried to catch the tight skin around his bellybutton with his teeth.

Micah was amazed to see these two playing with each other. He wasn't disgusted by what he was seeing. Instead, he had a greater understanding of why they worked so well together, why they were so attuned to each other. Micah had made love with many women, but never felt the close bond that Jude and Toryn obviously shared.

Jude's laughter was cut short as Toryn's eager mouth found his hard cock. Micah moved the camerata a bit to the side so he could see Jude's face as his lover grabbed him and tucked his tongue into the slit at the tip of Jude's shaft. The captain's hips lifted off the bed as he urged his navigator to take more of him and Toryn eagerly complied, teasing him with a tracing around the massive head, then down the length. Taking the captain in his hand, Toryn lowered his mouth over him and took him deep, all the while applying pressure with his cheeks as he began to move his head up and down.

Finally Micah's hand moved to the controls, but it was only to adjust the audio switch so he could better hear the loveplay between the two bounty hunters. Jude moaned as Toryn swallowed him and Micah could see Toryn working Jude's hard-on. He lifted his head and, starting at the base of the massive shaft, brought his hand up as he gripped tightly and turned his wrist back and forth to increase the pleasure. Up, down, up, down went the rhythm of his hand until Jude howled in agony. Toryn stuck out his tongue and slapped Jude's cock against it again and again, then licked just the crown, swirling his tongue all over it.

"Don't you dare come," he heard Toryn command Jude. "We're not done with you yet."

Chapter Two

ꟿ

As the words left the navigator's mouth, Micah saw who "we" was. Delia appeared at the bottom of the bed, watching Toryn as he pleasured the captain with his mouth. Micah sucked in a breath at the erotic tableau the three lovers presented. Delia, fully clothed in her flight suit and torso armor, while Toryn leaned, naked and voracious, over Jude's thick erection. The hungry look on her face told Micah that she wouldn't remain clothed much longer. She would have to join her lovers.

As Toryn perched on his hands and knees over Jude's cock, Delia climbed on the bed between his spread legs. To Micah's amazement, she began to nip at Toryn's butt cheeks, then brush the flesh with her tongue to soothe the sharp sting. He watched as she moved her face to his crease and began to lick him there. She spread his cheeks and lapped at him, liberally coating his opening with her saliva as Toryn groaned. When Toryn lifted his head again, Delia stepped back and watched as he went on his haunches over Jude's massive hard-on.

Micah knew what was going to happen, knew he should turn off the compuscreen, but he just couldn't flick the switch or look away. His own cock swelled in his breeches as Jude reached down and held his rod steady, letting Toryn use his powerful legs to hover over that enormous penis. The navigator leaned forward, resting his hands on Jude's chest so he could lower himself onto the rock-hard shaft. Micah watched in disbelief as the thick rod disappeared into the tiny puckered hole. He squirmed in his seat at the sight of that huge erection disappearing into Toryn's body, then shivered as Delia climbed on the bed behind Toryn and ran her hands down his spine. Toryn trembled as Jude's cock rested inside him and Delia delicately touched him. As she drew back, Toryn used his arms and legs to power his body up that gorgeous cock, only to slide back down. Delia crouched at the bottom of the bed so she could see the massive organ being taken into Toryn's hole.

"Oh Toryn," Delia whispered. "Do you have any idea how beautiful you are? I love to see that big hard cock disappear inside you. How does it feel? Can you take all of him?"

The air was full of the sounds of the lovers' moans. Micah knew that from his position on the bed, Jude would be able to watch his cock slide up into Toryn's powerful body.

Micah wondered what that would feel like to watch another man take his shaft inside him. He imagined that it would be so different from making love with a woman, with her soft, supple channel that would guide him inside. He'd have to press his way in past the puckered rosette, the opening clutching him tightly, reluctant to accept his hard-on.

What would it be like to have all that raw power above him as his partner sank down on him? Micah knew that he was bigger than most men. Was he too big to be accepted into a man's body? Some women even had trouble taking him, so what would it be like for a man?

A movement on the screen drew him back to the captain's chamber. He looked on as Toryn drew himself up and off Jude's cock only to go on his hands and knees beside him. Jude sat up and went behind Toryn, running his finger up the crease of his ass.

Toryn's body accepted Jude's massive cock again and then the only sound was that of flesh slapping flesh as Jude began to pound into him. Micah could see Jude's heavy sac swinging with every stroke, then hear the sound of his body as it slammed against Toryn's, sending his rod deep, deep into Toryn's channel.

Micah didn't even remember undoing his breeches, but he was sitting, shaft in hand. As Jude thrust into his navigator's ass, Micah roughly ran his fist up and down his own erection, with a grip that was tight, almost painful. In tandem with Jude, he threw back his head and howled as his orgasm came down on him. On and on it went, his body shaking from the force of it as he watched Jude's body seize in ecstasy, pumping his cum into Toryn's body. Jude pulled out and threw himself beside Toryn.

Wiping his hand on his breeches, Micah tucked his spent penis back inside. The material of the breeches would absorb and eliminate any foreign material that it came into contact with. *That's handy in a situation like this,* Micah thought wryly as he reached to turn off the compuscreen.

No can do, his brain said as he heard what Delia was saying to Toryn.

"Turn over, Toryn," she said with a laugh as she rose to her feet. "I know you didn't come yet and that beautiful big cock is not going to be wasted." Toryn groaned, but Micah could see he obeyed quickly, probably eager to see what Delia had planned for him.

"I'm sure two big, strong fighters like you can take a little more. I just need to get out of this flight suit."

As the two male warriors looked on, Delia reached up and took hold of the catches on her torso armor, flicking them open to remove the armor and throw it aside. Grabbing the zipper pull, she slowly began to tug it across her chest from shoulder to waist, the sound echoing in the silence. Micah could see the two on the bed, watchful as wild *feringas* as they took in the scene before them. Even the sound of the zipper made their bodies stiffen, their cocks harden. They knew what was going to happen next.

"You remember what's under this suit, don't you, boys?" Delia shot at them as she parted the upper section of the suit to reveal her succulent breasts. "Nothing!"

Micah dropped his hand to his lap, resting it on his renewed erection, resigned to the fact that there was no way he would be able to turn off the screen. He would just have to hope the captain understood or, better yet, that the captain never found out.

Right now the captain had more important things on his mind as he crawled off the bed and knelt in front of Delia. As he went to his knees, she placed her hands on Jude's shoulders, letting him unlace her boots one by one and tug them off. He yanked off her socks and threw them aside before hauling her to her feet and peeling the flight suit from his comrade, revealing every luscious inch of that toned body.

Micah's cock crept back out of his breeches. The beautiful bounty hunter was indeed naked under her suit. Micah watched as the captain ran his hands slowly up Delia's legs, conveniently finishing with his thumbs touching her pink and swollen lips.

"Oh, you're so very ready for us, aren't you?" Jude said, smiling, taking control from Delia. "You're so swollen. Were you thinking about this as you watched Toryn and me?"

Delia nodded her head, obviously unable to speak.

"Maybe one of us could fuck you from behind while the other takes you from the front. Would you like that?"

She nodded again, her body swaying, only her lover's arms keeping her upright.

"Well, if you're going to take on both of us, I should definitely prepare you."

Delia's body began to shake.

"Toss me that lube," Jude said to Toryn.

Toryn grabbed a tube from the bedside table and threw it.

The captain swept it up as it landed on the floor at his feet. "You need to turn around so I can get you ready for us."

Delia turned and presented her back to him.

"Bend over," Jude said.

As she complied, he flipped the cap and squeezed a bit of the lubricant onto his middle finger. Snapping the lid shut, he threw the tube back on the bed. Running his finger down the crease of Delia's backside, he coated his lover's little pucker, then put his finger inside to make sure whichever hunter entered her there would be able to slide in easily.

Micah could see that Jude's erection was enormous and so ready to be inside Delia. He looked on as the captain left her and climbed back on the bed beside Toryn. The two men watched as Delia stood at the end of the bed, hunger etched on her face. It was Jude who called to her, tempting her.

"Look at us. Perhaps one of these big, powerful cocks could slide into you from the front and the other could slide into you from the back." Jude paused, as if giving her time to consider. "Maybe you should let me take you from the back. Toryn's cock is much bigger around and I don't know if you could take him inside you that way. But my cock is so long that it would reach way up inside you and maybe you couldn't take that either. Think about it this way—you win no matter how we take you.

"Why don't you come and climb on top of me, darling," he playfully taunted. "You know how far inside you I can reach with this," he added, running his hand up and down the length of his cock, lingering on the bulbous head. Toryn laughed. In the security bay, Micah grabbed his own cock and slid his hand up and down the solid length.

"Why would you want that skinny little rod inside you?" Toryn scoffed.

Jude howled with laughter at the absurd reference to his enormous cock. It may not have been as big around, but he knew it would certainly fill her a lot deeper.

"You know I can fill you like nobody else," Toryn continued. "Climb up here and let me stick this big cock inside you. You know you can't wait any longer."

Micah knew Delia couldn't wait any longer as she climbed right up on the bed and crawled onto Toryn's lap. That was the easiest way to take him and even that was going to be hard, really hard—just like Toryn. He held his shaft steady as she lowered herself onto him. As Delia bent forward, her hands on his chest, he surged up into her.

From his vantage point in the security bay, Micah saw Jude climb off the bed and come around to the bottom where he stood watching Toryn and Delia make love. He was astounded at the trust these lovers had in each other, the way they shared their bodies and their pleasure. He envied their closeness.

As a wolfish smile crossed his face, Jude grabbed the lube and anointed Delia's little opening. Clambering back onto the bed, he rose over her and slid his cock into her ass. Micah shivered when she screamed—a long, very loud scream, but certainly not one of pain, rather one of unimaginable carnal delight. His cock ached for release, eager to be serviced.

He had resigned himself to his status as a voyeur. If the other bounty hunters found out and were angry, then so be it. There was no way he was going to miss a minute of their loveplay, for loveplay was what it was. The way they took something elemental and earthy and changed it into something rich and feisty intrigued him. The way they talked to each other, the way they playfully taunted each other, encouraged each other, pleasured each other seduced him.

Then the two men began to move and Micah grabbed his cock tightly as Toryn pumped into her from beneath and Jude pleasured her from the back. It was obvious from her cries that she was almost delirious from the dual pleasure. It was incredible to see how the three lovers fell into a rhythm that allowed them to move in synch.

He couldn't take his eyes off the screen as Delia went over first with a shudder that led to a high, keening cry as the double assault triggered her release. Toryn pumped into her, crying out in relief and Jude was last, pounding into Delia, throwing his head back as he shot his essence into her.

Micah swiveled his hand up and down his erection, slipping his palm over the crest to smooth his pre-cum over the head and down the shaft. Just a few more strokes and he shot off as the others finished their erotic dance of love.

In the captain's quarters, Jude eased himself gently from Delia's body and fell onto the bed beside Toryn. With a sigh, Delia flopped forward onto Toryn's chest.

Toryn gently caressed her back. "That was pretty intense," he said.

Raising her head off Toryn's chest, Delia spoke through a yawn. "I think that the longer we're all together, the better it gets." Jude just lay there, his eyes filled with warmth as he watched Toryn and Delia.

Up until now, Micah had had a hard time seeing these three as lovers, especially Jude and Toryn. He'd always thought the stories to be exaggerated, but now that he'd unexpectedly been party to what went on in the bedchamber, he knew these bounty hunters were tough but loving and caring as well. Now he could see why they were so good at their job—all aspects of their lives together were based on absolute trust.

After a few minutes, Jude sat up and swung his legs over the side of the bed. "I'll go get the shower chamber ready," he said quietly.

Delia sat up and, placing her hands on Toryn's chest, lifted her body to let his cock slide free. With a kiss to his belly, she climbed off the bed and held out her hand to him. Laughing, he took hold and let her pull him to his feet.

Micah watched as they disappeared through the door that led to the shower chamber. The bounty hunters of *The Renegade* were famous, but the shower chamber on the star cruiser, designed by Toryn, was more famous, with its multiple showerheads, hidden recesses and multi-level seats for any kind of loveplay. Micah had only once had a glimpse of it and was intrigued by what could happen there. He was sitting, still staring at the empty screen, when Jude reappeared in all his naked glory and stood in the doorway.

"I'll meet you on the bridge in half an hour, Micah. I'll send Delia to take over security detail. You can turn the screen off now."

Micah's jaw dropped. Busted!

Chapter Three

ᘓ

Micah had no choice but to wait for Delia to come and take over for him. He wasn't sure what he would say to her or if he should even say anything. He felt guilty about having been caught watching their lovemaking, but the more he thought about it, the more he realized that it was no accident that the screen had been left on. For some reason, Jude had set it up so he could watch the lovers, but Micah wasn't sure why.

About twenty minutes later, he heard footsteps in the corridor, then a pause while the sensors read her DNA before the door swished open. Luckily, he'd had enough time while waiting to get himself all tucked back in and tidied up.

There was no need to turn around to know it was Delia—her unique scent preceded her. Coming up behind him, she put her hands on his shoulders in a friendly way just like she always did, but this time he shivered. He had never before been so affected by her scent and her nearness, but he had never watched her making love with the other bounty hunters before either.

"We wanted you to see the three of us together," she said quietly before he could speak. "What do you think about what you saw? Did you enjoy it?"

Micah wasn't sure what to say, so he decided to be honest with her. "I've never seen a man make love with another man before," he said.

"And…" she prompted.

"And it made me realize why Jude and Toryn work so well together."

"What do you mean?" Delia quizzed. She seemed curious to hear his reply.

"I could see the absolute trust they had in each other while making love and I see that same unconditional loyalty when they're working together. They have no doubts about each other and have the utmost faith in each other."

"What about when the three of us were making love?" she asked.

"You want me to be honest?" Micah said.

"Of course," she replied.

"I was stunned when I realized what was happening. I tried to make myself turn off the screen, but I couldn't make my body obey."

"Did you find it disturbing to see the three of us together?"

Another odd question, Micah thought, then he laughed. "Disturbing? Not really. I was so turned on that I came twice, or maybe it was three times, just watching you guys. Then I realized how much I envied what the three of you have, the closeness that flows into the way you work together, the way you hunt together. I realized that I wanted to be part of something like that." He laughed again. "I don't mean just making love with two other people. I also want the same kind of trust that you have in each other."

Delia stared at him for a long moment. Finally, hands on hips, she spoke. "One of your soul mates is right under your nose, but you already know that, don't you?"

She could tell by the set of his mouth that he was going to deny it, so she raised her hand. "Don't bother to tell me otherwise. You know it's true."

"That may be so, yet it doesn't get around the fact that Layla is just too young for me."

"Ah, so you admit it," she said, and then she smiled. It was an I-know-something-you-don't-know kind of smile.

"What?" he said, looking at her uneasily.

"Your life is about to get a lot more complicated," Delia said, slowly nodding her head.

Micah knew not to take Delia's predictions lightly. All the bounty hunters had sensor implants, but she was one of the few whose abilities went beyond even their heightened capabilities.

"This next mission will draw together you and your soul mates."

Before he had a change to ask her to elaborate, she made a flicking motion with her hand to shoo him out of the control seat and took his place.

"You'd better hurry. Jude's waiting for you on the bridge," she reminded him as she turned to the bank of compuscreens. Shaking his head, he walked away, still unsure of what had just happened. Maybe the captain would let him in on what was going on.

As Micah stepped out of the transport chamber and onto the bridge, it was obvious that Jude was getting right down to business. Even before the panel closed, the captain was striding toward him, a shiny black cartridge in his hand.

Micah's pulse skittered like it always did when he saw the infocartridge. It meant that he was being sent on a mission and all the background data would be stored in that slender box. Once underway, he could listen to everything the information managers of *The Renegade* had found to prepare him for the job. Their title was "information managers", but in reality, they were the best spies in the galaxy.

"You're heading to S'Leng 3," the captain informed him as he handed over the cartouche. Micah knew that Jude would give only the barest details of the mission. The slim cartridge that he was sliding into a slot in his torso armor would have everything else he needed.

"That planet is barely within this galaxy. What in Jobin's name is on S'Leng 3?" Micah asked.

"Not what, who," Jude clarified. "King Feldan's son, Prince Denyan, is on S'Leng 3."

"Prince Denyan? I remember seeing him when he was just a kid, but King Feldan never talks about him."

"That's because they had a ferocious argument years ago. Denyan left Tantor over it and ended up on S'Leng 3. His father wanted him to take a major role as heir to the throne, but the prince wanted a life of his own, a life that he'd choose, not one dictated by his father or a group of advisors."

"So why am I heading to the backwater of the galaxy?"

A very nasty look came over Jude's face. "One word—Brachan."

Micah frowned. "The Redelian leader? I hear he's furious at the way you got him to turn over Delia and Toryn."

Jude laughed, but it wasn't a nice laugh. "The Redelians aren't noted for their pleasant disposition."

Micah snorted at Jude's comment. "I'd say they're better known for their nasty temperament and razor-sharp claws."

"Don't forget the ten-inch barbed prong that masquerades as a dick," Jude added.

Micah shuddered just at the mention of the barbarous appendage.

"The situation is serious. We've got a double problem here, Micah. Brachan still holds Feldan's daughter, Princess Tresta, and he believes the king was party to my plan and has sworn revenge against him."

"I thought the king just got caught in the middle."

"That's not what Brachan thinks and King Feldan's afraid the barbarian will take out his anger on his family. Our sources tell us that Redelian soldiers are actively searching for his children to allow their leader to carry out his vengeance."

"So what's your plan for me?"

"Some of the hunters are escorting the king's children to safety, where they'll remain until Brachan is dealt with. Even though King Feldan hasn't seen the prince for years, Denyan is still his son. He wants to make sure that he's all right and he be given protection if needed."

Micah snorted. "And that's my job? I'm to check on the kid?'

"Don't forget that you haven't seen him for years," Jude pointed out. "He's not a kid anymore. He's twenty-four now."

"Sounds like a pretty simple job to me. I go to S'Leng 3. I check on the kid—I mean, young man—then I come back here."

"Don't get too cocky. Brachan has spies everywhere. I suspect even on S'Leng 3. So keep your wits about you and your ass covered."

"Thanks for the warning, captain," Micah said as he swung round to the transport chamber.

"And Micah."

Micah looked back over his shoulder. "Yeah?"

"Good luck."

The portal to the transport chamber slid open and Micah stepped inside.

* * * * *

As the little speeder pod zipped through the sky, Micah thought back over his conversation with Delia.

What the hell did she mean about me and my soul mates? Sometimes her ability to see inside people or to see what's going to happen is downright scary to say the least.

But now he had to stop thinking about all that and focus on the mission. He was to head to the planet S'Leng 3 to check on King Feldan's son Denyan, make sure the guy was okay and, that accomplished, head back to *The Renegade*.

On the surface, it looked like the job should be a piece of cake, but in Micah's experience any mission that looked to be neat and easy very seldom was, especially with a creature like

Brachan in the mix. He felt off-kilter, like something wasn't quite right, but all the holographic readouts from the pod were normal and his sensors picked up nothing unusual, so he tried to relax.

Feeding the coordinates for S'Leng 3 into the autopilot, he pulled out the cartridge and slid it into a slot in the control panel. As the monotone voice began to impart the necessary information, Micah settled back in the seat.

According to the "information managers" aboard *The Renegade*, Prince Denyan lived in Kingoolia, one of the largest cities on S'Leng 3, and worked at a place called The Mandate. They hadn't been able to ascertain exactly what the prince did at The Mandate, nor were they able to provide a current image of him. He'd been estranged from his family for so long that any photopics they had were woefully out of date.

Micah wondered what kind of business it was with a name like that. It sounded like some type of government facility with—he shivered—perhaps people in positions of authority. He didn't deal well with authority.

What do you want to bet that Prince Denyan is some kind of government official, or worse yet, a number cruncher? Great! I can hardly wait to meet the boring little fleeb. Why couldn't Jude have sent one of the newer bounty hunters?

Micah knew if he went to *jergaspeed* he could be in Kingoolia in half the time, which meant he'd be back aboard *The Renegade* even sooner. So he fed in the coordinates that would take him directly to the city and flicked off the autopilot. Reaching above his head, he pulled a lever, then gripped the control yoke as the tiny pod hurtled off. The distance passed in a blur of kaleidoscopic colors that bombarded the cockpit and, as always, Micah gritted his teeth, his body pressed back against the seat. He hated *jergaspeed,* but with a planet like S'Leng 3, out on the very fringes of the galaxy, it was the most expedient way to get there.

It wasn't until the windshield displayed the rainbow of colors that indicated the termination of the jump that he felt he could finally relax, a little. None of the other bounty hunters had this special feature, but he had complained so loudly and so often about his dislike of *jergajumping* that the tech wizards aboard the ship had added that little color feature to appease him.

Who knew all that complaining would actually pay off?

It didn't make the jumping any more pleasant, but at least he knew when it was coming to an end.

He heaved a sigh of relief as the docking bay of Kingoolia appeared dead ahead. As soon as he hailed the ground crew and was given the number of the berth for the pod, he sailed the craft along the entry tunnel reserved for small vessels and found himself in a cavernous area full of massive shelves. As the craft had emerged from the passageway, a holographic path leading directly to the assigned cradle had appeared in front of him. It was just a matter of steering the pod along it, backing into the little holding bay and flicking off the power.

Before he even had time to open the cockpit, a small platform came speeding through the vast hall and stopped directly in front of the landing cradle. It remained immobile as Micah slid back the canopy and climbed out. It continued to silently float as he walked to the edge of the berth. Two handles telescoped up each side of the platform, then clicked into place. He stepped on and was whisked along a corridor to land out on the street in Kingoolia. The transplatform was programmed to go no further, so when Micah stepped off, it dropped its handles and slipped back down the passageway.

As the bounty hunter stood and looked around at the crowded streets, he got that feeling again, that spine-tickling one that let him know that something wasn't quite right. A surreptitious visual search and sensor scan of the area revealed no hidden threat, but Micah just couldn't slough off the feeling.

It wasn't a sense of malevolence but rather one of being touched, a gentle caress along his backbone, a graze at the nape of his neck. Then it was gone.

Shaking his head to clear it, he stood watching as vehicles sped past, some at ground level, but most in the air above the skyscrapers. The dull blue sky was like a living creature with all the vehicles darting to and fro and it seemed like the entire landscape of Kingoolia was made up of tall buildings. The whole scene was disconcerting for someone like Micah who spent most of his time in the sky, but once this job was over, he'd be back on *The Renegade*.

"Need a lift?" he heard a voice say. Drawn from his reverie, he saw a speederform, which was basically a platform with a seat for the passenger and one for the driver.

"Sure," he said, strapping himself in before giving the address for The Mandate.

Micah quickly discovered that there were no rules of the road in Kingoolia. It was every man for himself, or actually every creature for himself, as vessels of all shapes and sizes, piloted by beings from all corners of the galaxy, whirled around the speederform. Yet it just zipped through the traffic, flying over and under other vehicles and around corners without so much as a hint of slowing down. Eventually it glided to a stop and Micah stepped off.

This street was quiet—few people, little traffic. Too quiet and Micah wondered why. As that prickling sensation skittered down his spine, he gently eased a weapon from his torso armor. His sensor implants still picked up nothing, but he knew that someone was following him. A movement across the street caught his eye and he swung around, knife in hand.

Chapter Four

ꙮ

The speederform driver caught sight of the blade and threw his hands up. "Hey man. It's just a Kingoo cat lookin' for something to eat."

Micah relaxed and slid the knife back into his armor.

The driver relaxed and drew his hands down. "You sure are jumpy."

Micah gave him a thin smile. "Comes with the job."

The man nodded slowly, then, looking past Micah, asked, "You certain this is where you wanna go?"

"What do you mean?" Micah followed his gaze and noticed the posters. He moved closer and stared at the pictures of the scantily clad men. He studied them as if he couldn't understand what they signified.

In all his imaginings he'd never thought The Mandate would be just that—a place for men to meet other men, a gay club.

He burst out laughing.

"Not what you expected?" the driver surmised.

"Not really," Micah said dryly, not bothering to elaborate.

"You can't get in yet, you know. Nothing'll be open. It's too early."

The bounty hunter looked around at the empty street, finally seeing the other clubs, none of them open for business yet either.

"Can I take you somewhere else?" the man offered.

"No. I'll be fine," Micah returned as he paid the fare. With a nod, the driver set the speederform in motion and took off.

With The Mandate not yet open, Micah had some time to kill. Maybe he could find a place to stay. He knew that whoever was following him was close by, so he decided to go about his business and let his shadow come to him.

While scouting the neighborhood, looking for a hotel, his mind went back to Prince Denyan and the mission. He'd been so surprised finding out about The Mandate that he hadn't thought about the implications. Micah had assumed that King Feldan's son was a government official, but that certainly wasn't true.

What was the prince doing working in a gay club? As soon as the place opened for business, he would find out for himself. Right now Micah intended to catch a shadow.

Using one of his assortment of alternate-identity cards, he booked a room at a hotel a few blocks from the club. Taking the transport tube to the third floor, he walked down the emergency stairs to his room on the second floor. Micah had found that, in his line of work, it always paid to be cautious. Know all the exits and get a room just above the ground floor.

Putting a thumb on the entrypad in the wall, he stepped to the side and pushed the door open with his foot. No one was inside, but he already knew that. No spine-shivers. Nevertheless, since he was a man who took no chances, Micah checked out the accommodations thoroughly and, finding nothing out of order, was able to relax.

He hoped his stalker would soon make a move. He was tired and hungry and the bathroom had a big tub that looked very inviting. Someone must have salvaged some stuff from Old Earth because it was one of those ones with the fancy feet—plenty long enough to cradle his six-foot-three-inch frame. *The Renegade* had only shower chambers, so a bathtub was a luxury and he was eager to get naked and soak in it. He desperately wanted to put his clothes in the renewalchamber but knew he'd have to wait until he'd dealt with the anticipated intruder.

He didn't have long to wait.

The bathroom door was ajar, the tub filled with hot water as if he were enjoying a peaceful soak when he heard the door of the room being opened.

From his spot behind the bathroom door, he heard the trespasser make his way across the bedroom. He frowned at the sound of shoes hitting the floor and a zipper being lowered, then assumed battle stance as the interloper began to push open the door. Micah let his shadow enter fully and, as he heard him step over to the tub, put out his arm and slammed the door shut.

Prepared to tackle the intruder, he stood dumbfounded at the sight of the naked woman. And not just any naked woman, but Layla. He knew he should look away or throw her a towel, but she was just so damned gorgeous that he couldn't think straight.

Then *she* went on the offensive.

"What in Jobin's name do you think you're doing?" she shouted. "You scared the hell out of me!"

"What in Jobin's name am *I* doing?" Micah fired back. "You're the one who's been tailing me all over Kingoolia? How did you get here and why were you following me in the first place?"

"I hid in the back of the speeder pod and I followed you thinking maybe I'd get a chance to seduce you," she cried, grabbing for a towel.

The small room fell silent as she realized what she'd said.

Micah smiled and swiped the towel before she could get it.

"Seduce me?" he asked. As a naughty smile took hold of his mouth, he threw the towel to one side and advanced on her. "You want to seduce me?"

"I haven't been able to stop thinking about what happened on Chend. I want more of that. I want you."

He shot his arm out and pulled her to him. Turning her around, Micah pinned Layla against the counter and whispered, "Don't ever think that I don't want you." He licked the shell of her ear, pressed his erection against her ass. "You could seduce a man just by walking into a room. You tempt me every time you walk by and I catch your scent. But I'm trying to be sensible. For Jobin's sake, I'm thirty-six years old and you're just a baby."

He got the spine-shivers when she leaned back against him. "Does this feel like the body of a baby?" She spun around. "Does this look like the body of a baby?"

Putting his hands on her shoulders, he leaned his forehead against hers. "I just want to do what's right."

She sighed and stepped back. "Is this really about the difference in our ages or is it about something else?"

He said nothing.

Layla put her hand on his chest, stroking him tenderly. "Tell me what you're thinking."

"Do you want the truth?"

"Of course."

"When I was inside you, I knew exactly what you wanted, what you liked. I knew exactly what to do to please you and I've never felt that with another woman. Everything was for you, for your pleasure and I was certain that I'd found my soul mate."

"And you know I felt the same link to you."

"I just never expected to find a woman that I would have a connection with, then for her to be so…"

"Young," Layla finished for him. "Micah, forget the age thing. Do you want to be with me? Do you want to see where our connection takes us?" She waited for his answer, worrying her bottom lip with her teeth.

"I really can't resist you, you know," he declared, smiling.

"Good," she replied, taking his face in her hands. "I'm glad you finally came to your senses."

Then she kissed him and Micah felt her releasing all the frustration she'd held inside when she'd thought he didn't want her, felt her showering him with the sheer joy of just being together.

Drawing back, she ran her hands from his forehead down his cheeks, savoring the rough feel of him, the sharp jut of his cheekbones. With one finger, she traced his lips, laughing when he stuck out his tongue to touch it, then shivering as he sucked it into his mouth, drawing her into the gentle rhythm of seduction.

She laughed as he reached down and swept her off her feet, carrying her out of the bathroom and into the bedchamber, where he let her slide down the length of his body.

"I need to feel you skin to skin," he breathed, reaching up to remove his torso armor.

Layla swatted his hands away so she could flick the release catches and haul it off him. Underneath, the jacket of his flight suit hugged his body like a second skin, while the tight leather breeches only emphasized the size of his powerful thighs and commanding erection. Running a finger along his shaft made her shiver as she imagined all that power inside her, filling her, pleasuring her. She was delighted to feel an answering shiver run through his steely body.

Nothing like a big, bad bounty hunter, ready to be seduced.

Layla felt his eyes on her as she put a hand on the zipper of his jacket and took hold of the tab, pulling it across his chest, from shoulder to waist, bit by bit revealing his golden skin. She felt his quick intake of breath as she bent and put her tongue to him, licking a line up the newly bared flesh. His body was so beautiful, enhanced rather than marred by the scars on his chest. Those marks showed how he had become the man he was, the kind of life he had led.

Going to her knees, she began by playfully grabbing at the skin around his bellybutton with her teeth, her tongue following to sooth the tiny bites. When he arched his back, she knew he was encouraging her to take what she wanted from him, do what she wanted to him.

Reaching up, she stroked his abdomen. It was taut, so taut, that it was like caressing warm *classen*. Dragging her hands down his body, she placed one on top of the huge bulge in his breeches. Even through the leather, she could feel how hot he was, like the forges on Shartantarus.

"I can't take much more of your torture," Micah croaked. "If you're punishing me for letting you believe I didn't want you, then I don't blame you, but for Jobin's sake, take pity on me."

Layla just smiled up at him. She wasn't finished with him yet. Rising to her feet, she took hold of the two sides of his jacket and pulled them down his arms and off, letting it fall to the floor beside them.

Her tongue flicked out and tickled his chest, lingering on his stiff nipples. She worried first one then the other, gently disciplining him for his reluctance to reveal his feelings. It wasn't really punishment, just a prolonging of the inevitable, but she wanted to make him wait, like he'd made her wait.

She ran her hands along his pecs, sliding them up his taut skin, across his wide shoulders. Her thumbs sought his nipples, flicking the firm tips, drawing her palms into place so she could rub them over the rigid points. They were as hard as the little jewels she'd picked up on her last mission to Balgorial.

"Oh, they look so painfully tight," she said sympathetically. "Let me make them feel better." She laved one tight nub with her tongue and she could tell by the way he was squirming that he wasn't feeling soothed at all. Good! She wanted him squirming. Squirming and oh-so ready for her.

"Let me try the other one," Layla said, putting her mouth to his other nipple as she leaned her body into his. His groan made her smile.

She wanted him to know that she was going to tease him and keep teasing him until he begged for mercy yet again.

There was no way she was going to let up. Not yet.

Layla tugged the hard nipple with her teeth, gently, but enough to make his cock jump. His erection slithered along her belly, getting even longer and harder. Letting go, she nibbled down his chest, tickling him in her downward journey. She was delighted to hear him laugh.

That was what she wanted their lovemaking to be—erotic and naughty, but joyous. Even his navel was sexy to her and this time she couldn't resist painting a circle around it with her tongue before she pressed inside and lapped him there as well.

She knew he must be reaching the end of his tether, so, standing up, she gave him a shove. As Micah fell back, Layla climbed on top of him and sat on his belly, letting him feel how wet she was. She made sure to wiggle around so he knew that she was eager to have him inside her, slick with her desire for him. Rocking back and forth, spreading her juice on his skin, marking him. Leaning forward, she gave him a quick kiss before she pushed herself back and off him.

"Those breeches look mighty tight on you, my dear hunter," she said mischievously. "Why don't I just help you take them off?"

Undoing the placket, she spread apart his black leather breeches and was delighted to find nothing underneath but his gorgeous penis, which immediately sprang out, eager for her attention. Bending down, she flipped the bands on one of his boots and pulled it off. Micah laughed as she lost her balance and landed on her backside, his boot grasped firmly in her hands.

"Are you all right?" he asked, getting to his feet.

She sat speechless, lost in the sheer beauty of his body. His long, dark hair hung to his shoulders, framing his tanned face. He had the look of a dangerous man and Layla knew from experience that was true. She'd seen him in action and he needed no weapons to defend himself; his body was enough of a weapon without them.

He was tall and his arms were roped with muscle. His shoulders were so wide that she wondered how he found torso armor to fit. He was definitely not a man she would want for an enemy, but he was incredibly loyal, having proven that time and time again with the other bounty hunters. She knew it was all those things that drew her to him. He was beautiful to look at, but he was strong and fiercely devoted to his friends.

And she couldn't wait to have him inside her.

"Are you all right?" he asked again. Rather than answer, Layla threw his boot to the side and smiled up at him as she put her elbows on the floor behind her and spread her legs wide open for him.

It was his turn to stare as she lay below him, pink center glistening with her juice. He still couldn't believe that this beautiful woman had followed him all the way from *The Renegade* with the express purpose of seducing him. He didn't know what he had done to deserve this incredible good fortune and this incredible woman but he was enjoying every minute of it. Thank Jobin she had refused to give up on him.

She appeared to be such a delicate woman, but he'd sparred with her a few times on board the star cruiser and she'd held her own even against someone his size. That was the key to her success as a bounty hunter. People continually underestimated her and he'd seen many men who'd made that mistake because she was small and because she was a woman. Those men were now spending time in brigs all over the galaxy. Layla was very good at what she did.

He couldn't help but grin as he looked down at her. She seemed to be very good at seduction as well. But he could tell by the gentle rivulet of cream nestled between her folds that although she may have thought she was seducing *him*, she was just as affected as he was.

"I'm just fine," she answered, feigning an air of nonchalance. "But you really need to take those breeches off for me. Did I tell you how much I like the way they hug your body?"

Micah shook his head slowly.

"Did I tell you how much I like the way they hug your nice big cock?"

He shook his head again.

"Well, I do," she said, gazing up at his erection, framed by the opening of his breeches.

"You look so hungry. Are you hungry for me?" she teased.

Two could play at this game, Micah thought as he ran the flat of his hand up and down the length of his cock. He knew she was suffering when she started to clamp her legs together in a vain attempt to give herself some relief.

"Ah, ah, ah. No fair. Keep those legs open for me," he teased. "You're the one who started this seduction."

She spread her legs again.

"I thought you were going to help me take these breeches off."

He saw her body quiver. Then she smiled up at him, daring him, tempting him.

"I'd rather watch you. I'll be able to see everything from here and I don't want to miss a thing. Sit down and take off your other boot and socks," she commanded.

As Micah sat down on the bed, he knew Layla didn't realize that now he had an even better view of her luscious slit. He could not wait to put his mouth there and lap at her. As he leaned down to get rid of his other boot and socks, he was delighted to see how ready she was for him.

She was suffering too.

Throwing his stuff aside, he rose to his feet and stuck his thumbs in the waistband of his breeches. He made sure that he pulled them down very slowly, forcing her to wait a bit longer until he was naked for her.

He pulled one foot free, then the other and stood to his full height, letting Layla see exactly what was in store for her. He saw her legs were shaking from her arousal and that little rivulet had begun to gently run down her slit.

Micah couldn't wait any longer to taste her, so he went to his knees in front of her. Before she could protest, he placed her legs on his shoulders. Sliding his hands down her smooth skin, he raised her ass, bringing her right to him.

Her taste exploded in his mouth as soon as he put his tongue to her. She was so slick and delicious as he licked her, laving her plump lips and spreading her juice. He suckled her labia, drawing them into his mouth, gently prodding her clit with the tip of his tongue. She wept more cream, more delicious cream that he greedily lapped up.

"Oh, Micah," she sighed as his tongue slid into her very core.

His hands tightened on her ass as she tried to escape the all-consuming pleasure of his mouth.

But he held fast.

As Micah felt the first of the heavy contractions around his tongue, he dragged her even closer to his mouth, allowing him to push even deeper into her channel. Now, instead of pulling away, she thrust her cunt at him, crying out for the relief only he could bring.

Her channel grabbed him, powerfully at first, as her orgasm burst through her. He held her fast as the tremors grew less and less intense, letting her release flow through them.

As the last flutter died away, he raised his head to look at her and wondered if that was the same expression that he had on his face. He hoped he reflected the same look of wonder and surprise, of contentment and satisfaction.

He didn't move, just held there, savoring the rightness of what was between them.

Then she laughed.

"And what part of my loving makes you laugh?" he asked curiously.

"It's definitely not the loving that makes me laugh." she returned with a smile. "It's the circumstances. I've spent weeks thinking about what it would be like to make love with you again. I imagined making love in exotic locales, in beautiful bedchambers, in Jude's infamous shower chamber, yet here we are lying on the floor in some second-rate hotel and all you had to do was put your mouth to me and I was gone. It couldn't get much better than that."

"Oh, I wouldn't say that," Micah replied as he gently set her legs down from his shoulders and grabbed a pillow from the bed.

She looked at him quizzically as he handed it to her.

"Here, put this under your head."

He watched as Layla swung the pillow beneath her head. "Do you trust me?" he asked quietly.

"Completely," she said honestly.

"Good. Then hold on tight," he said, lifting her hips up off the floor and keeping her legs in position against his thighs. Her back was bowed like a bridge, but he knew that she was in top physical condition so the position was more unfamiliar than uncomfortable. As he took the weight of her body with his hands, he moved forward and began to slide into her from a kneeling position.

Layla cried out, and he stopped.

"Are you all right? Am I hurting you?" he asked, concern in his voice. Her eyes were full of tears and he was afraid he had misjudged her ability to take him in this position.

"You...feel...so...good," she finally managed to say. "I don't know if I can bear it."

"I'll try to make it easier by coming into you a bit at a time," he assured her.

She had to laugh. "I don't think that'll help. You're just so big."

Those words made him even more determined to be inside her. And made him harder. And longer.

"Can you take your weight on your legs for a minute?" he asked.

Layla nodded and he let go of her with one hand, seeking her clit with his thumb, feeling her swollen and ripe for him, her little hood stiff and eager for his touch. He pressed hard, then pulled back and began to rub in a circle. He flicked her clit and slid his cock in a bit further.

Micah could feel his shaft rubbing against the snug walls of her vagina as he slowly pressed his way inside her. As he circled her nub with his thumb, he could feel her juice bathing his cock.

She was such a contradiction. Small and feisty on the outside, yet so rich and ripe for taking him inside her.

He just kept pushing into her body, his thumb making those lazy circles. Finally, he felt his balls nudge against her behind and knew he was all the way in. As her hot, juicy channel cradled his cock, he could sense her connection bumping his brain, telling him what she wanted, telling him to take hold of her ass and start moving.

First he pulled out unhurriedly, drawing his cock back along her oversensitive passage, tantalizing her, tormenting her. Then he gently pushed his way back in, forcing her body to accept him, to hug his shaft. She was so tight around him.

He kept up the gentle, swinging rhythm until she growled at him.

He knew what she wanted, but he wanted to hear her say it.

"Enough, Micah. Fuck me!"

He was so willing to obey, filling the room with the sounds of his flesh smacking against her as he rammed into her, Layla moaning as she met each thrust.

Their link let Micah please her as she needed to be pleased, sometimes hard, sometimes more gently, but always filling her long and deep. At the same time, she was giving him what he wanted. Grabbing his cock tightly with her inner channel until he groaned, then backing off when he was ready to detonate. Calling to him tenderly before again commanding him to fuck her.

Suddenly she cried out and he held still inside her, sharing the first telltale flutterings of her orgasm. The pulsing grew in intensity until he felt her squeeze hard one last time and he knew he wouldn't be able to hold off any longer.

With his hands on her ass, he hauled her to him as closely as he could, gripping her as the ultimate pleasure careened through her body. But it wasn't just through his *body* she was linked—it was deep within his whole being. It was as if his body had become hers and he was sharing the waves of her release. They sang through his veins, rippling along his skin, shoving him into his own climax.

Micah felt his cum jet into her, wave after wave of power surging into her, filling her, and he couldn't move. He wanted to stay there forever, with that soft, sleek passage cradling his cock, the delicate aftershocks trembling along his shaft.

But her murmured protestations reminded him of her less-than-comfortable position. He gently let her legs down and his cock slipped from her body.

Chapter Five

ꟈ

Micah laid his body between her outstretched legs, resting his head on her soft belly, running his hand along her arm. He needed to touch her, to keep connected to her. When he felt her stroking his hair, he lifted his head and licked her belly.

She giggled.

He looked at her quizzically. "Did you just giggle?" he asked.

"Maybe," she said.

"I thought I just heard you giggle," he said.

"Maybe I did," she said. "And maybe I didn't."

"No, I'm pretty sure that I just heard one of the bounty hunters from *The Renegade* giggling," he stated. "I wonder if that bounty hunter happens to be ticklish."

As soon as the words left his mouth, Layla began to struggle beneath him. Micah crawled up her body, pinning her hands above her head.

Then he went on his knees and gently sat on her belly. "I think our Miss Layla is ticklish. Keep your hands above your head and don't move."

He wanted Layla to surrender, knowing it could only lead to pleasure.

Drawing his hands down the sensitive skin of her arms, he caressed a path to her breasts. He squeezed them lightly, pushing them together to lick the valley he made in between. She moaned and he smiled.

"Hmmm, your breasts don't seem to be very ticklish, but I wonder what would happen if I took one of these tight little nipples and bit down on it?"

She struggled to push herself away from him, but he was too heavy. "Oh, you're afraid that you might like that too much, aren't you? It was fine while you were the one doing the seducing, but now it's my turn, little girl."

He felt her body go rigid when he called her 'little girl', but he'd decided that he wanted to provoke her, to get her going so he would get a chance to tame her. With her fiery temper, he wanted to feel that heat when he surged into her again.

"You have very pretty nipples, little girl," he said as he leaned down and licked one.

She moaned again.

"Ah, you thought I was going to bite you and you're disappointed, aren't you?" he teased. "Did anyone else ever tell you what pretty nipples you have?"

This time his question was followed by a pinch with his teeth. He felt her body lifting beneath him, but he knew it was to get closer to him, not to escape.

"The other one seems to be begging for me to put my mouth on it as well. Would you like me to do that? Or maybe you're too ticklish for that?" he said mischievously.

"No," she ground out.

"No, you don't want me to do that? Are you sure?" he said, frowning.

"You know what I mean. I'm not too ticklish for that. Just put your damn mouth on me," she cried.

"Oh, I'll put my damn mouth on you and I'll make you scream," he said firmly.

Micah kissed his way from the tip of one breast to the other, pausing to nip her sensitive skin as he went. Even though he knew Layla wanted him to hurry, he perversely ignored her moans of disappointment as he lingered in his journey. He heard her sigh as he finally took her other nipple and worried it with his teeth, biting just a bit too hard, pulling just a bit too much, tempting just over the line.

Letting go, he scooted down her body, propelling himself with his arms and turning his head so his rough cheek scraped her tender skin. Her bellybutton distracted him, making him nibble around it, then biting across her waistline and licking down her pelvic bone. That bone led him to the crease where her leg met her hip, so he used the tip of his tongue to paint a line right to her clit.

Then he surprised her by standing and pulling her to her feet. Placing his arms at her back and behind her knees, he lifted her up and carried her to the bed, setting her down so her legs hung over the edge.

"Remember how I said I was going to put my mouth on you and make you scream?" he whispered.

She nodded.

"That would be now."

Going to his knees, he lifted her ass just enough to slide his hands flat underneath and raise her up a bit, then he touched her with the stiff point of his tongue, forcing it into the very center of her clitoris and pressing hard. She tried to squirm away from him, but he held her firmly in place as he stopped pressing and began to flick his tongue back and forth over that ultrasensitive core. Using his lips and tongue, he sucked the swollen flesh into his mouth and flattened it between his lips, worrying the tender flap, knowing that it wouldn't hurt her, would just drive her crazy.

Lifting her bottom a little higher made it easier for him to taste her where she was so wet and creamy. He stuck his tongue inside and tickled the roof of her passage, delighted when she tightened her muscles and tried to trap it. Pulling out, he licked and licked at her slit, grabbing her fleshy labia alternately with teeth and then with lips.

She was close to coming, so he jammed his tongue inside her again, felt that betraying quiver as she exploded into his mouth, screaming as she came. As the juice wept onto his tongue, he lapped at it, tasting how ripe she was for him. After the final few tremors, he set her bottom on the bed and let her watch him as he licked his lips, savoring the last bit of her cream.

She lay quietly, but Micah knew she was planning.

A very naughty look came over her face and she pulled herself up into a sitting position.

"Stand up," she said, and he did so, putting his cock right at mouth level.

Uh-oh – payback time.

"So you think I have very pretty nipples do you, little boy?" she teased. Calling him a little boy was like teasing a wild creature – she knew something would happen. She couldn't tease a wild beast and not expect to pay the price. That was a lesson she'd learned on Chend. Although the price had been her surrender. Total surrender in return for incredible pleasure.

Putting her hands to her breasts, Layla grabbed her nipples with thumbs and forefingers and rolled and pulled them. "Do you like to watch me play with them, baby?" she taunted playfully. She watched Micah's cock stiffen and creep toward his navel, a drop of pre-cum glistening on the massive head.

"Maybe you'd like this better, sailor," she sassed as her hand snaked down to come to rest between her legs. Her forefinger slid out and reached under the hood of her clit, rubbing circles of pleasure while he looked on. He flexed his hands at his sides and she knew he wouldn't be able to stay still for long.

She smiled like a cat as his breath hitched in his throat. He couldn't tear his eyes away.

"Hold onto your cock so I can put my mouth on it," she ordered.

Micah reached out and tried to hold his rod steady for her. As Layla leaned forward, she saw his hands become more and more unsteady the closer she got. Finally, pulling her hand from between her legs, she placed her hands over his, imprisoning them beneath hers. Then she bent forward and touched the tip of her tongue to his tiny slit. She felt his hands quiver.

"You must be ticklish too," she said, laughing.

"I'm sorry I teased you," he said. "Take me in your mouth. Please."

She let him drop his hands, then held on and licked his length. With one hand, she swiveled up and down his cock, increasing her grip bit by bit. Sticking out her tongue, she slapped his heavy cock against it. It made a solid, fleshy sound.

"Oh sweet Jobin," he cried. "Have mercy, Layla."

She swallowed him whole. Sweet torture as she drew in her cheeks to apply suction to his cock. More torture as she moved her head up and down his length. When she felt he was close to letting go, she pulled back, ignoring his groan of frustration.

As another little drop of cum appeared on the tip, she leaned forward and circled her nipple with his cock. She traced a line between her breasts with his shaft before pushing them together to ensnare his cock in between.

With her head down she could lick the crown as his rod lay trapped there. Her breasts pressed tightly together, she let him move his shaft up and down. He put his hands on top of hers, squeezing her breasts even tighter together and clutching his erection in their sensual grip.

Layla loved it. He made her want to attempt things that she'd never done with other lovers, but at this very moment she needed him inside her, so she pushed his hands away.

"I have to have you inside me. Right now."

"Lie back," Micah said, and Layla let her body fall back on the bed so he could take her legs behind the knees and step in close to her.

She felt his cock nuzzling her entry, then sliding in and she groaned with him as he pressed fully inside her. He began to move, pushing her up the bed, so she grabbed the covers and held on.

As Micah slid in and out of Layla's body, he couldn't help but smile at how her seduction was progressing. He wasn't sure who was seducing whom, but he loved it nonetheless.

Looking down, he watched her body taking his cock inside, her beautiful pink lips swallowing his erection. Micah loved the way she groaned as he slid into her, so he made a series of slow glides that swept back out in leisurely retreats. Shifting the pace, he pumped with short sharp spurts that pummeled her until he couldn't hold back and began to hammer into her, letting her feel the full fury of his size. Her sharp cries signaled her imminent release, her orgasm clutching his body, drawing out his own, throwing it to the surface. Sliding his hands under her legs, he lifted her, surged into her, roaring as it came down on him, knowing by the mind-blowing force of it that she was sharing with him.

Micah stood for a moment, then as his penis slid from her body, crawled onto the bed and pulled her into his arms.

They lay in silence until Layla spoke. "I think I really like where our connection takes us. I like knowing that I'm your soul mate."

Micah thought for a moment. "That's how you followed me so easily from the speeder pod, isn't it? You didn't even need your sensor implants."

Layla pulled away from Micah and sat cross-legged beside him. He put one arm behind his head and looked up at her. She cocked her head, drawing her thoughts together before she spoke. "Jude and the others seem to share the same kind of link. I don't know how or why it works and it's not the same for everyone, but eventually each hunter finds the one or ones who are connected to them."

She studied his face. "Delia once explained to me about the three of them. I know that their link is so strong that unless they're off the ship they usually try to 'disconnect' to give each other some privacy. It's not great having someone rummaging around in your head or in your feelings all the time. 'Sometimes you just have to shut everything down and go on autopilot,' is how she explained it."

Micah considered her explanation. "She said I would find my soul mates on this mission," he said. "Do you think there's someone else to complete the circle?"

"Oh most definitely," Layla answered, grinning. "I keep having visions of you and me making love and there's someone else with us. I've seen his face and he's gorgeous. I'm not sure who he is, I just know you'll meet him very soon."

"You have no idea who it is?" Micah asked.

Layla shook her head. "But every time I have a vision, I get the feeling that he's someone who will become very important to us."

"When did you figure out there was a link between the two of us?"

"A few weeks after I came on board *The Renegade,* I realized that I knew where you were anywhere on the ship and I knew exactly what you were doing. If you went wheels up, I knew the instant you were off the ship. It was as if a cord had snapped and I felt incomplete until you returned."

"You knew where I was and what I was doing?" he asked.

Layla couldn't meet his eyes. "Yes, for me our connection was strong even then," she said.

"Strong enough to let you find me wherever I was? Whatever I was doing?"

"Yes."

"How does it work? Do you just have a vague sense of where I am and what I'm doing?"

"Well...not exactly."

"What do you mean—'not exactly'?"

"Well, I mean that I don't have just a vague sense of where you are."

"Then how do you know where I am or what I'm doing if you don't have a vague sense about it?" But as Micah asked the question, the answer had already started to reel around in his head. She had the same heightened abilities as Delia. "You see me, don't you?"

Layla nodded.

"I'm sorry," she said, "but our link is so new that I have no idea how to control it. The pictures just come flooding into my head and sometimes I try to shut them out."

"Sometimes," he said.

"Yes. Sometimes," she said, blushing.

"What don't you try to shut out?"

Layla looked away.

"Layla, what don't you shut out?"

She mumbled something.

"Tell me Layla. What do you like to see?"

"Sometimes I like to see you eat. I don't shut that out."

"That's all right," he said.

"Sometimes I like to see you sleep. I don't shut that out."

"I don't mind that either," he said.

"Sometimes I see you in the shower. I don't shut that out."

Micah smiled wolfishly. "You see me in the shower. What am I doing?"

"Oh, you know...washing."

"Do you like to see me in the shower? Do you like it when I soap my hands, then rub them over my body?" he asked softly.

Layla nodded.

"Do you like it when I soap my hands and rub them across my chest?"

She nodded again.

"What do you really like to see me do when I'm in the shower?"

Layla looked at him, tears forming in her eyes. "I've invaded your privacy and I'm sorry," she said, looking away.

"Layla," he called. She refused to look at him, so he sat up on his haunches and, taking her face in his hand, turned her to look at him. "I'm not angry that you watched me. In fact, if you look down you'll see that the whole idea really excites me."

Layla looked down to see his arousal vying for her attention.

"Now tell me what you like to see me do in the shower."

Looking right at him, Layla spoke, "I love to see you cross one soapy hand over your chest and wash first one armpit, then the other. I love to see those same lathered hands as you run them over your chest and down your belly so you can grab your cock. I can see you with my eyes open or closed, so I can't escape the vision as you run both those hands up and down that massive hard-on."

"What do you do while you watch me?" Micah asked softly.

"I put my hand between my legs and pleasure myself while I watch you," she said, gaining confidence. "Sometimes I reach into the drawer by my bed and get out my mancock and use it."

Micah raised his eyebrows at her revelation.

"Yes. I bought it soon after I joined the crew of *The Renegade,* soon after I met you, to be exact. You didn't seem interested and since I couldn't stop seeing you in my head I had to find relief somehow, so one time when we had a short layover, I visited a shop and bought one."

"What kind of mancock did you choose?" he asked curiously. "Or, should I say, how did you decide which one to choose?"

"Do you really want to know the truth? Do you really want to know how I chose it?" she said boldly.

"Yes, as a matter of fact I do," he said, leaning forward and brushing her lips with his own.

With one finger, he traced a shivery path between her breasts. "I want to know if you tried them all out before you bought it."

Taking one nipple with thumb and forefinger, he pinched ever so gently. "I want to know how big it is and if you can fit it all inside you."

He began to torment her other nipple. "I want to know if it feels as good as my cock inside you because for some crazy reason I find myself to be insanely jealous of your artificial cock."

"You don't need to be jealous," she said, laughing. "I'd seen yours often enough when I watched you in my head, so it was easy to pick out one that was most like yours."

Now it was Micah's turn to laugh. "So does it feel as good as mine?" he said, teasing her.

"You know it doesn't. There's nothing that feels as good as your cock inside me and you know it. Did I mention that the salesperson said very few people buy that particular model?"

"And why is that?"

"It's too big for most woman and they find it very uncomfortable," Layla said innocently. She watched as Micah's cock lengthened at her words. She loved her mancock, but she loved having the real thing inside her so much more.

"Do you want me to finish telling you about what I like to watch you do when you're in the shower?"

"I don't know if I can hang on that long," he said, groaning.

"I love to watch your hands on your erection, pulling it. I like it when sometimes you're rough with your cock and I wondered if you knew I was watching you. Did you know?"

Micah shook his head.

"What were you thinking about?"

"Maybe I'd be thinking about a woman."

"Who?" she asked.

"You," he said succinctly.

"Well, while you and your hand were practicing safe sex, I would use my mancock and watch. Sometimes I could make myself wait and I would let myself come at the same time as you did. I felt like I was with you, but it wasn't enough, not nearly enough."

"Is this enough?" Micah said as he grabbed her around the waist and hauled her across his legs. He knelt with his legs tucked under him so she put her hands on his shoulders and gently lower herself onto his penis, loving the feel of that hard bar being swallowed by her body.

"Isn't this better than your mancock?" he said as he pushed up into her.

Layla leaned forward and took his bottom lip with her teeth so she could nip at it. She traced the sensitive underside of his top lip with her tongue, then traced around his mouth with it. She gave him a gentle kiss, slipping her tongue inside, touching his tongue with hers, letting him chase it around in his mouth. Pulling back, she stared into his eyes as she used her legs to lift up off his cock and slam down.

"Isn't this better than your hand?" she asked as she repeated the movement, drawing her body up until he was poised at her entry, sliding back down until she took him completely inside.

Then the teasing was gone and they lost themselves in one another. The up and down rhythm, the slippery sounds of his cock inside her, the passionate kisses to fuel the flames, the hum of his body as she started to come, the fire as he joined her.

This time when he lay back and pulled her into his arms, they slept.

Chapter Six

ꟸ

Layla woke to the gentle touch of Micah's hand stroking her hair.

"I'm sorry to wake you," he said, "but the sun's gone down and I need to go to The Mandate to check on the prince."

Layla stirred beside him.

"I won't be long. As soon as I make sure he's okay, I'll be back. Maybe we'll keep the room for a few more days and check out Kingoolia. There must be stuff to do here, places to visit, or we could just spend the next few days in bed."

Layla shook her head.

"You don't want to stay here?" Micah asked.

"No. It's not that. I just have a feeling that it's not going to be as easy as you think. Something's going to happen. I can feel it."

"Ah *freck*! I really didn't want to hear that. I keep thinking the same thing, but I figured it was just me."

Micah climbed out of bed, picked up his clothes and boots and padded to the bathroom. Standing in the doorway, he turned and looked back at Layla. "I'm just going to take a quick shower, then head over."

After throwing his clothes in the renewalchamber, he pressed a button on the wall-mounted control panel to activate it. Everything would be clean and fresh by the time he was finished in the shower. A jab at another button and the door of the shower chamber hissed open, sliding shut after Micah stepped inside.

He looked around. It was very ordinary, not at all like the one aboard *The Renegade* with its shelves and secret recesses, its toys and multilevel showerheads, although this one did have a low ledge along one wall.

He'd love to share the shower chamber in the captain's quarters with Layla. He'd never actually used it, but he'd seen it and could imagine lots of ways to utilize its incredible features.

As the hot water streamed down his naked body, Micah felt the air around him shift. He could sense Layla leaving the bed and approaching the bathroom. Each time they made love, the connection grew stronger. When he'd first picked up that she was shadowing him, right after arriving on Kingoolia, it had only been an awareness, an awareness that must have been awakened for him by their time together on Chend. After making love with her this time, that feeling had intensified, had deepened, heightening his link to her.

He shivered in anticipation at the hiss of the door to the shower chamber, felt her hands on his back, little nibbles at the skin of his shoulder blades. Reaching past him, she took the soap and lathered her hands, then ran them, fingers down, over the smooth skin of his back to his firm ass. Micah tensed as she ran one finger down the crease of his butt. He wasn't sure how he felt about being touched there.

"Does that make you uncomfortable? When I touch you there?" she said against his back.

"I'm not sure how I feel about it," he said. "It just feels odd. No one has ever put their hand to me there."

"Do you want me to stop?" Layla asked. "I will if you want me to."

Taking a breath, Micah shook his head. He felt her go to her knees behind him, caressing his ass cheeks, alternately biting then licking. She put her tongue to his little puckered hole.

He jumped.

"Relax," she said. "I won't hurt you."

Micah tried to relax, but it was difficult with this beautiful woman on her knees behind him, her tongue at the furrowed flesh, pressing at the very center to lubricate the opening.

Then she replaced her tongue with her hand.

One finger slipped inside and it was bliss.

Micah closed his eyes and threw back his head at this first penetration. He had no idea his anus would be so sensitive. That one digit, that one unhurried motion, seemed enough to bring him to his knees. Or so he thought, until she began to slide her finger in and out. A simple enough action, but not at that constricted flesh. The added sensation was incredible, exquisite. Her devotion to his pleasure wrung a deep moan from him.

But she wasn't finished torturing him yet. Layla turned her hand, palm up, and began to stroke the top of his channel, a leisurely caress over ultra-responsive tissue.

Micah couldn't believe what she was doing to him. It was as if his whole being was centered on that digit, like his body could melt into a pool of molten ecstasy. He soaped his hands and, grabbing his erection, ran them roughly up and down its length, then just one hand over and over the head. He pumped his cock while she finger-fucked him, the combination pushing him over the edge.

He howled his release.

As he leaned forward and put his head on the wall, he felt her remove her finger.

"Are you okay, Micah?" she asked softly.

"I'm not sure," he said, turning around.

"I'm sorry. I thought you might like it."

"I think that's the problem," Micah explained. "I loved it. Too much. I loved the idea of something inside me, pleasuring me. It was wonderful."

"What are you thinking, Micah?"

"That I'd love to feel a man's cock inside me. Is that too strange?" he asked.

"Did you start thinking about it after you watched the other bounty hunters aboard *The Renegade*?" she questioned.

"How did you...? Oh, you saw me, didn't you?" Micah said with a grin.

"Oh yeah. I was still on the ship as well. I never went ashore with the others. I've got to tell you that scene will be getting extra playtime in my head. I was afraid I was going to wear out my mancock during that episode."

"You watched me and pleasured yourself at the same time?"

"I couldn't shut the pictures off, so I figured I may as well enjoy them." She looked at Micah, wanting to gauge his reaction to her question. "Did you like to watch Jude sticking that huge cock of his into Toryn?"

Micah nodded at the memory.

"What do you think that would feel like, all that raw male power inside you?"

Micah was quiet for a moment, but finally he said, "I think it would be incredible. I think I would love it, but I don't know why I'm even discussing it because there's no man that I'm interested in making love with."

"That's about to change," Layla said.

"Well, whether it happens or not, I need to get ready and go check on the prince." Reaching out, he lifted her chin and placed a kiss on her lips. "But first, I think I have some unfinished business with a certain little bounty hunter."

Lathering his hands, he placed them reverently on her breasts, lightly massaging the tips with his palms. She arched her back as he slid up and over her shoulders, lightly stroking the nape of her neck and that sweet spot just below the ear.

As he drew his hands along her jawline, she threw her head back, letting him trace a path down her elegant throat, caressing a trail along her slick skin and back to her breasts.

"Your breasts are so sensitive," he whispered, pinching her tight little nipples, pulling and tweaking them until she leaned forward and lightly bit his chest.

He laughed. "I think you like it when I play with them."

"You know I do."

"Well, I think I'd like it better if you turned around."

Layla complied, obviously knowing her pleasure was guaranteed.

Cocooning her with his body, Micah reached around and cupped her breasts, teasing her nipples with his thumbs. Running his hands beneath, he made a V with his fingers and slid them down her chest, down her belly, to her nest of curls.

She moaned. Micah hoped it was in anticipation.

"Oh baby, do you need me to help you?"

He took her answering sigh for a yes and moved one hand lower to find her silky slit.

She was so wet, so slippery, so juicy.

His long finger slid around her clit, circling the tight knot of flesh, then traveling between her swollen lips to enter her. With that naughty digit, he took her cream and spread it up and down her cunt, coming to rest on her clitoris. Micah flicked its hood, then traced the underside of that cap of flesh. Back and forth, back and forth, each stroke driving Layla further into the curve of his body, against his solid cock.

His erection lengthened and crept up her back, seeming to take on a life of its own in its quest for entry.

"Put your foot on the ledge," Micah murmured, against her ear. "That'll make it easier for me to slide in and you'll be able to take me nice and deep."

He shared the shiver that rippled through her as she lifted her leg and set her foot on the ledge. Her body knew that thick rod was going to be pressing its way inside her. Immediately.

Micah grabbed his cock and guided it into her body. She was so ready for him.

He didn't need any connection to know what she wanted. She wanted exactly what he wanted—a fast, furious fuck. And he gave it to her. He pounded into her, his chest slapping her back, the sounds of flesh meeting flesh filling the shower chamber, to be quickly joined by the cries of their combined release.

Micah held onto Layla tightly, trying to keep his cock inside her. She fit so perfectly in the crook of his body, fit so perfectly in many ways. He didn't want to let her go, but he knew that The Mandate would be open by now and he did have a mission to take care of.

Sighing as his spent erection slid from her body, he reluctantly set her away from him and quickly showered. Micah pressed the release button inside the chamber, waited as the door hissed open, then stepped out. Another jab on the wall button kept the door from closing while he grabbed a towel from the warming rack. As Layla stepped out, Micah caught her up in the cozy towel.

She melted against him, cradled by the heat of the cloth and his body, practically purring as he dried her off. When he was done, Layla took another towel and tenderly smoothed the soft material over him.

Micah cradled her face in his big hands and kissed her, then with obvious reluctance said, "I need to go now."

Layla stepped away as he retrieved his clothes and boots from the renewalchamber. He loved the look of disappointment on her face when he pulled on the black leather breeches, tucking his cock away. A sigh escaped her as he slipped his arms into the jacket then zipped it shut. Socks and boots came next.

She followed him into the bedchamber and lay down on the bed, propping the pillows behind her, watching as he bent to pick up his torso armor.

As Micah clicked the shoulder catches shut, he began to wonder why Layla was being so acquiescent about his mission to check on Prince Denyan. Bounty hunters often worked in pairs. *Why didn't she ask to come along?*

"So I guess you're just going to lie there and rest and wait for me to come back?" he asked, suppressing a grin. He knew very well that when he left, she'd be right behind him. But he didn't need her help to check on the young prince.

Feigning a yawn, Layla said, "I'm worn out. I'll just stay here until you come back."

"Well, I'll get out of here and let you get some rest. But I need a last kiss from you," he said, getting on the bed and straddling her. As he cupped her head in one hand and drew her forward, he slid the other into a secret slit in his torso armor and removed an object.

Layla was too busy worshipping his mouth to notice what was happening. When she grabbed his head to deepen the kiss, Micah seized the opportunity to snap the cuffs onto her wrist.

Being a bounty hunter, she was well acquainted with that sound.

"You take these off me," she cried, struggling to get out of them, but Micah easily swung her arm back and attached it to one of the bars of the bed. "Let me go! Let me go!"

As Layla tried to hit him, Micah took her free arm and licked the sensitive underside.

"That's not going to work with me," she said through clenched teeth, trying to buck him off her legs.

"Then maybe this will."

Leaning forward, he took her breasts in his hands and set his mouth to one, sucking her nipple and flicking it with his tongue. She continued to struggle, but Micah could feel the change in her as her rage turned to need and she pushed up into him, trying to get closer. That was when he knew he had to get up or he wouldn't be able to stop. And he did have a mission to complete. So he climbed off the bed, pulled the sheet over her luscious body and headed for the door.

"Wait, Micah," she called.

He turned. "Don't worry. We'll take up from there when I get back."

She shook her head in frustration. "That's not what I'm talking about. Take me with you. This just doesn't feel right to me. You might need my help."

He gave her a wide smile. "Ah, you're worried about me. You needn't be. I just have to make sure his highness is okay then I'll be right back and we can take up where we left off."

"Have you forgotten about the Redelians?" she said, tugging on the handcuffs.

He just shrugged. "There's been no information to indicate that they're anywhere near S'Leng 3. I'll be fine. I'll be back before you know it." He blew her a kiss, then pushed a button on the wall panel. The door opened and he disappeared. He knew Layla would be fuming in frustration at being left behind, but he didn't want her along on his trip to The Mandate. It would be very difficult for her to blend in with the clientele of an all-male nightclub. Besides, a quick reconnaissance to satisfy himself that the prince was fine and his job would be done. She was fretting over nothing.

Chapter Seven

ഇ

Micah hailed a speederform outside the hotel and gave the driver the address for The Mandate. This time when the taxi dropped him off at the door, the sound from inside the building was deafening while the lights above the entry portal throbbed in time to the music.

The club was most definitely open for business.

As he stepped inside, Micah wondered how in Jobin's name he would ever find Prince Denyan in this mass of humanity. The strobe lights inside the club gave an air of unreality to the whole scene as the throng of men seemed to be continually frozen in place, then released in quick succession. The dance floor writhed like a living thing as couples and threesomes and moresomes touched and kissed and fondled, all to the quick-freeze effect of the lights.

People sat around tables, laughing and drinking and hoping for more. Darkened booths, clustered around the walls, seemed filled with patrons in various stages of undress. As Micah passed close to one booth, he noticed some customers sitting on the seats and others on the table. A quick glance confirmed that those on the table were having their cock sucked by those who were seated, while those who were sitting had their own cock in hand.

Taking a look around, he realized that it was going to be much more difficult than he'd thought to find the prince. This didn't seem like the kind of place where he could just wander and ask questions.

So Micah decided to do what he did best—bide his time and attempt to stay in the background. Using his sensors, he scoped out the room but didn't pick up any danger, just a healthy dose of lust and arousal.

He could see a large horseshoe-shaped bar on the other side of the room, so he made his way over. Not an easy thing to do in a space crammed with so many men. As he pressed his way through the crowd, he wondered what it was about his ass. First in the bar on Chend and now here. It seemed like everybody wanted a feel as he wound through the mob. Finally extricating himself, he squeezed in at the bar.

"I'll have a Swarzinian beer," he yelled above the noise.

The bartender nodded and Micah swung round to survey the scene.

A tap on the shoulder a few minutes later had him turning to find his drink being passed to him. Micah paid, raised the bottle to his lips and took a long, cold swallow. Clutching it, he moved past the group gathered at the bar, hoping to find anonymity in the shadows.

But the darkness held more than a place to hide, much more.

A customer leaning over a table being fucked from behind. Another with his rod in the mouth of a supplicant while a small group looked on, hard-on in hand.

He stepped back and turned away, but the image was still there, burned in his brain. Only now he was on his hands and knees in front of an incredibly large cock, one hand on it and the other hand on his own. His tongue licking, his hand pumping himself.

Micah shook his head trying to erase the vision. He had to stick to business. Pushing his way through the throng, he finally found a table near a small darkened stage. He just wanted to finish his beer, check on the prince and get the hell out of there.

Suddenly the lights dimmed, the music stopped abruptly and a shiver rippled down his spine. He turned as a single spotlight began to illuminate a figure onstage. The crowd moved toward the light and Micah got to his feet and found himself standing just below the lip of the platform.

Waiting.

Then the spotlight flashed on full, revealing the man.

Micah felt like he'd been kicked in the stomach. He was drop-dead gorgeous, wearing a beautifully tailored Old Earth tuxedo, black boots and a crisp black bow tie. The frill of a white dress shirt peeped out above the V of the jacket. The jet-black suit had obviously been custom-made for him as he was too tall and too muscular to be able to find a suit like that in any shop.

The crowd was absolutely silent, everyone drinking in the masculine beauty of this man.

And Micah knew he'd found Prince Denyan.

"Good evening, gentlemen," the god said in a voice that made Micah think of dark rooms and hot, slick skin.

Still no sound, still that hushed expectation from the crowd.

Then the music started, a pounding rhythm to accompany those graceful hands as they began to undo the buttons on the tuxedo jacket one by one, revealing the pristine white shirt beneath. Micah couldn't tear his eyes away as the man finished undoing the buttons and pulled the sides of the jacket apart, his wide shoulders bunching beneath the material as he shrugged out of it, letting the garment drop to the floor. The men in the crowd began to howl.

The shirt was next, with its unbelievably tiny buttons. One by one they were undone until a thin sliver of the massive chest beneath was unveiled.

He turned his back on the crowd, revealing long dark hair caught back in a thick braid. Micah was afraid he was going to leave the stage, but he just stood motionless until the noise subsided. As the crowd fell silent, he reached up and, tugging the band from the bottom, unraveled the rope of hair, leaving it hanging loose down his back.

As he turned back to face the audience, a young man appeared on stage, carrying a silver pail. The prince grabbed a chair from the side of the stage, brought it to the front and turned it backward. He sat down, held onto the chair, then leaned back and closed his eyes as the young man began to pour the water down his powerful chest. The water streamed down taut flesh, slicking his shirt to that golden skin. The man gently poured some of the water through Prince Denyan's long dark hair, where it cascaded down and formed a pool on the floor behind him.

Micah had never seen anything like it. The music was relentless in its driving, throbbing beat and the waves of lust pumping through the room were like a living, breathing being. It was as if the water fanned the fire of this fierce desire, not quenched it, and Micah wanted this man with an unbelievable hunger.

The pail empty, the young man strode away, leaving the figure sitting in the chair. Slowly he rose, the shirt plastered to his body, and shook the water from his hair. Droplets went everywhere and Micah felt some land on his lips. The men in the audience began to shout and hoot. Micah licked away the drops and looked right at the stranger, meeting his eyes, and knew that this was the man in Layla's vision. This was the final link in their connection, the circle of three was complete.

Prince Denyan.

Hello, Micah. You've finally arrived.

Micah felt a jolt as the prince's words touched his mind for the first time. The link was so strong, so intense, much more so than his link with Layla. Maybe it was because he wasn't fighting it the way he had tried to fight his need for her. Maybe it was because she wasn't the big, hard male that Prince Denyan was. Whatever the reason, he couldn't wait to see what happened when they were together.

The prince flung his head back as the spotlight flipped to blue and the music changed. Another tune, another beat, but still throbbing and hypnotic.

Undoing the bow tie, Prince Denyan dropped it to the floor. He grabbed the two flaps of his shirt and peeled them back, his skin dripping with water. The shirt met the same fate as the tie.

He turned the chair and sat down to remove his shoes and socks. Rising to his feet, Prince Denyan undid the placket of the tuxedo pants. The men in the crowd may have been hollering, but Micah was holding his breath, waiting to see the beautiful cock hidden inside.

He was doomed to disappointment as Denyan slid the pants down to show a pair of tight white underwear. But it quickly turned to approval as the prince drew the pants over one foot, then the other and rose to his full height.

Because the water from the silver pail had not only soaked the shirt but the pants as well. Micah could see a very long, very thick and obviously very stiff erection through the wet, clingy material.

And he wanted it.

In his mouth, in his hand and—he shuddered—in his body.

Everything about Micah was too tight, watching Denyan. His own cock was aching and so very hard that he wanted to stroke it and give himself relief. He looked to the side and saw that the man beside him was going at it with no compunction, his hand down the front of his pants, roughly stroking himself, looking for release. Micah knew how he felt as his eyes turned to the show again.

While the music pounded, Denyan hooked his thumbs into the waistband of his whiteys and pulled them down over his hard thighs, down his long legs and off. The crowd went crazy, but Micah couldn't tear his eyes away from that shaft. It was like a bar of forged *classen* yet pulsing with a life beat, thick dark veins running its tremendous length.

He remembered Layla's finger penetrating his ass and how good it had been, but no way could he imagine what it would be like to have the power of that rod inside him. What if he were on his hands and knees with Denyan cradling his body from behind?

First the prince would run his hands over Micah's ass and down the backs of his legs, squeezing the flesh, claiming the body, and then he would put that gorgeous mouth on Micah's butt, nipping and licking his cheeks.

Would he lick his puckered flesh the way Layla had?

Would it feel as good?

He wanted Prince Denyan to part his cheeks and lick his crease, then put his finger inside and drag it in and out. Micah wanted the prince to cover him from behind, stretching his body up and over his own. Prince Denyan was at least two inches taller than he was, so he knew that gorgeous body would cover him completely.

Micah, you're not watching. Where are you?

Micah's head shot up.

What do you want? he shot back.

The prince was staring straight at him, six-foot-five-inches of naked male with a heavy cock that kissed his bellybutton.

I want you to watch and to want, bounty hunter.

You know I want.

Denyan stood in the blazing spotlight and ran his hands over his chest, squeezing his nipples and pulling them. The crowd roared in approval.

Do you like that, Micah?

Is that all you've got?

Giving his back to the crowd, the prince ran his hands down his ass, squeezing it, bending forward so the crowd could see his balls hanging between his legs.

Swiveling so his butt faced Micah, he spoke only to him. *That's where you're going to put your tongue and then maybe I'll let you put your cock inside me. Would you like to slide yourself in there?*

Do you think you can take all of me?

I'm sure I can take whatever you can give, and with that comment Prince Denyan turned, straightened and swept his hands over his torso, rubbing tantalizingly down his taut belly.

Micah's mouth went dry. He knew where those hands were headed. He rubbed the front of his leather breeches where his hard-on lay thick and throbbing.

The prince stood, sweat coursing down his body, the music pounding through the room. He moved his hands lower, driving the crowd into a frenzy of anticipation. His assistant appeared onstage again, but this time he had a small tube. As Denyan held out a hand, the young man squirted the lube onto his palm, then quietly turned and left the stage.

The spotlight changed to white, the music dropped to a low mournful jazz tune and Prince Denyan took his rod in hand. As if under some kind of spell, Micah unfastened his breeches and did the same.

Through the blinding light, his eyes unerringly found Micah and he began to fist his throbbing erection. Long, tight strokes that covered the whole length, a cupped hand massaging the crown.

This is for you, Micah. Each stroke. Each tug. Each one for you.

He watched the prince's face change and knew he was close, so close. Micah didn't bother with finesse. Never looking away from those eyes, he moved his hand. A few hard, tight strokes and he groaned his release. Onstage, the prince locked onto Micah's face as his cum shot up and onto his chest.

Next time I do that, I'll be inside you, was the message Prince Denyan sent this time.

You'd better be, Micah replied as he tucked away his cock and fastened his breeches.

The spotlight winked out as Denyan turned and walked to the back of the stage and out of sight amid the deafening applause of the crowd.

Chapter Eight

ꝏ

Micah waited a moment before turning and pushing his way through the throng. A huge blue man stood sentry at the doorway that led offstage. The bounty hunter's body stiffened as he prepared to fight to be allowed to enter.

As soon as he saw Micah, the burly guard stepped aside to let him pass. "I'm to let you through," he said.

Micah strode past him, stepping into a long narrow hallway with doors all along the left and right hand sides. Scanning the names on each door, looking to see which one bore Denyan's name, would take too long, so he just stood still and focused. Within a few seconds he was able to shut out the throb of the music from the stage area with its hoots and hollers from the crowd. The sounds of people's voices receded into the background and he let the prince draw him.

Stopping in front of a door at the end of the hall, he reached out and quickly pushed the handle down, shoving the door open. Prince Denyan was standing in the middle of the room, naked, gorgeous and hard.

"What in Jobin's name took you so long?" he barked at Micah.

Micah stopped and stared for a moment. He had no idea whether Denyan meant he'd taken too long to come backstage or whether he'd taken too long to get to Kingoolia, but it was a moot point now, for he was here and he was primed.

Turning, he flung the door shut behind him and hit the button to lock it. He leaned his forehead against the closed portal, his hands flat on the metal, and tried to regain his equilibrium. He couldn't understand the fiery need he felt for this man, but he knew he had to have him, now.

"You are so beautiful," Denyan said from behind him. "I wasn't prepared for how beautiful you would be."

"What do you mean?" Micah said, swinging around to face him.

"I've dreamed of you for years," the prince said. "I knew that one day you would come."

"How'd you know it was even me?" Micah said.

Prince Denyan walked over and put his hand on Micah's face.

"I knew."

Denyan undid the catches on the bounty hunter's torso armor, dropping it to the floor beside them. Next he pinched the tab on the zipper between his thumb and forefinger and pulled it across Micah's chest, exposing the golden skin. Micah had to shut his eyes as the prince licked every bit of flesh as it came into view. When the tab reached the end of the zipper, Denyan pulled it free, yanked the jacket of the flight suit apart and pulled it down his arms and off. Prince Denyan leaned down and swiped his tongue across a wide shoulder and up his neck, only to take the hunter's earlobe between his teeth and bite down.

Micah moaned.

Denyan grinned.

He set the tip of his tongue to the pulse of Micah's neck, feeling the strong rhythm, nipping his way down his pecs to arrive at the brown disc of one nipple. Prince Denyan stopped long enough to brush it with his tongue before continuing his downward journey. He dropped to his knees, only to get sidetracked by Micah's bellybutton. Once he placed his tongue in Micah's navel, he discovered that the tough, gorgeous bounty hunter was very ticklish. It was hard to believe that the famous Micah O'Brien had any softness about him.

Denyan sat back on his haunches to take stock of this man he'd been waiting for. To his thinking, Micah was a perfect specimen of manhood. They were of a similar height, which was unusual, for on all the planets he'd visited, he seldom found any man as tall as he was. His eyes were a beautiful blue with a clarity that seemed to look right through to one's soul. His nose was a bit long, but it fit his angular face. The top lip, a bit larger than the bottom, made Denyan want to take it between his teeth and nibble. Powerful muscles covered his chest, a testament to the life he led.

He looked like the dominant beast that he was.

And he was still wearing his breeches.

Denyan couldn't wait to remedy that situation.

"Are you done looking at me, Your Highness?" Micah said. "Because I need to be inside you in the worst way."

"I'm not done looking and I'm definitely not done touching," the prince said with a grin. He reached out and undid the bounty hunter's breeches, pulling them apart to reveal the tip of Micah's cock.

"Bingo. Commando," Denyan exclaimed, as he spread the breeches open. Delighted with his discovery, he leaned forward and licked under the crown and across the very tip. Micah's hands fell onto the prince's shoulders.

"Take them off me," Micah commanded.

Rising to his feet, Denyan grabbed a chair and hauled it over. "Sit down so I can take off your boots and socks."

As he sat down, Prince Denyan knelt at his feet. Micah licked his lips at the play of muscles in his back as he bent over to flip the bands on first one boot and then the other. Denyan pulled off the boots then the socks, leaning back on his haunches to watch Micah get to his feet.

"Now the breeches," the hunter ordered.

Prince Denyan quickly realized that the close-fitting trousers could not be tugged down, so he got to his feet, set his thumbs inside the waistband and shimmied them over Micah's hips and down his long legs. As he lifted each leg in turn, the prince pulled the breeches over his feet and off.

"I think I like you on your knees," Micah said, pushing down on the prince's shoulders.

Denyan had no trouble complying. Now all he had to do was lean forward and put his mouth right on that gorgeous cock. He felt Micah's hands in his hair, drawing him closer as he put his own hands on the hunter's rod and licked the tip.

The few drops of pre-cum were absolutely delicious, lingering for an instant on his tongue before he swallowed. The skin felt soft and supple as he plied it with long strokes, bathing it, savoring it. He had waited so long for this man to come to him that he wanted to enjoy every moment of their pleasure.

Pulling back, he put his hand on Micah's cock, sometimes stroking, sometimes rubbing over the crown so he could use the hunter's juice for lubrication. He couldn't wait to feel that heavy cock pushing its way inside him. He wanted to feel that first jolt that came when the shaft would push past the tightly drawn opening and surge into his inner passage. He wanted to feel Micah's balls slapping against him, signaling that his cock was as deep inside him as it could go. He wanted to feel the power of the bounty hunter thrusting inside him, dragging his rod back to the opening again and again until he wanted to cry for mercy or cry for more. He wanted to thank Jobin for giving him the connection to this man, but first he wanted to fuck him until neither of them could stand. Once he could wrest control from Micah. But he could wait. Maybe.

Take me in your mouth," Micah said.

Oh yeah, he could wait.

Prince Denyan complied and Micah slid right in. Relaxing his throat, he took him deep. It was the most luscious, the most succulent, the most savage of flavors and Denyan thought his head was going to explode. He could never have imagined the exquisite taste of him, a taste so fine, so rich and dark, so like the man.

For years he had dreamed about Micah, knew he was his connection, but it wasn't until his most recent visions that he was able to see that this would be part of their bond. He had always pictured Micah as being his mentor, not his lover.

Obviously visions don't reveal everything, he thought wryly, *or I would have gone looking for this man long ago.*

The prince drew back and, placing his hands between Micah's legs, forced him to spread his legs. He could feel the bounty hunter's speculative gaze on him. He suspected that Micah had no experience with a man, but in Denyan's mind that just made it all the more exciting. He knew that he would be Micah's first and, if he had his way, only male lover.

Placing his hands palms out, he ran them up the inside of Micah's thighs, the hair rough against his palms as he moved them up and down the powerful legs. From this angle he could see Micah's cock pointing to his navel, but he also saw his heavy balls hanging exposed.

"Spread your legs wider apart," he ordered. "I want to be able to get at your beautiful balls."

Micah complied, taking a wider stance and exposing himself to Denyan's eager gaze. Without preamble, the prince leaned forward and took one of Micah's balls into his mouth, sucking hard on it and licking it with the flat of his tongue.

"What in Jobin's name are you doing to me?" Micah cried, totally lost in the pleasure.

"Don't you dare move," Denyan said as he relinquished his hold on Micah's sac. "I've waited patiently for you to come to me and now I'm done waiting. So just relax and enjoy the ride."

Prince Denyan heard Micah laugh and knew there was no way the bounty hunter was going to be able to relax. Not with what the prince planned to do to him, to do with him. Reaching forward, he took Micah's balls in his hands and played with them while he licked up his cock.

"Do you like that?" he said, looking up.

"You know I do," Micah said through gritted teeth. Denyan wondered if he was anxious about what was going to happen between them.

"I'll let you take me first if you want," he said. "This is your first time with a man, isn't it?"

"Yes, but I want to feel you inside me."

Denyan stood and took Micah's hand and pulled him to the center of the room. "Get on your hands and knees," he said.

The bounty hunter dropped to the floor and went on all fours. Denyan got behind him and cocooned Micah's body with his own. He stayed there, letting Micah take most of the weight, knowing he was too heavy, but not caring. He could feel his cock setting itself into the crack of Micah's ass as if it already knew its final destination and he loved how good that felt, how right it was.

Reaching around, he pinched his lover's nipples, tugging them, giving them a little twist. When Micah moaned, Denyan bent his neck so he could bite the hunter's shoulder, hard. Leaning back a bit on his haunches, he ran his hands down Micah's sides, starting at his armpits and down his flanks and then he reached underneath and took hold of that massive cock.

"You are so hard," Prince Denyan whispered.

"I've been like forged *classen* since I saw you in the glare of the spotlight, but you already knew that, didn't you? That was part of your plan, to drive me crazy with want."

All the time Micah was talking, Denyan was stroking the hunter's cock, stroking and tugging and smoothing his hand across the head.

"You'd love to have me jack you off right now, wouldn't you?" Denyan said.

"I'm not going to last much longer anyway," Micah said stoically.

"Well, in that case, I'll just move on to the next step of your seduction," the prince countered.

He was sure he heard Micah groan as he began to caress his ass and down the backs of his legs, squeezing the muscles as he went. Micah shuddered. Denyan began licking the bounty hunter's cheeks and nipping him. When he felt him relax a little as he began to enjoy the gentle play, the prince wooed him by running his hands up his inner thighs and gently caressing his balls.

Are you all right?

Micah nodded.

Prince Denyan parted the cheeks of his lover's ass and found the little pleasure hole he sought.

Do you want me to keep going?

I want it all.

Prince Denyan set his tongue to the crack of Micah's ass and licked a path to his opening. He spat on his fingers and used the saliva to lubricate the hunter's puckered hole, then he feasted on the succulent flesh, licking and licking, dipping his tongue inside. He felt Micah's body jolt as he penetrated him with his tongue. As the bounty hunter began to move his ass up and down instead of remaining quiescent, Denyan became voracious in his need to please his lover, shoving Micah's cheeks apart and ramming his tongue into the hole.

Micah cried out and Prince Denyan decided to up the pleasure. Drawing back, he placed his finger at the entry and began to push inside. He could feel his lover tightening and it was so good that he didn't want to tell him to relax, but he knew he would never be able to put his cock inside unless Micah loosened up to accept the invasion.

"That feels wonderful, doesn't it?" Denyan said as he slid his finger in and out of the tight little orifice. He tried slipping his finger in with the palm up, then switching to slide in palm down, trying all ways to pleasure his lover. Looking down at Micah's beautifully sculpted back, Prince Denyan realized that he just couldn't wait any longer to be inside him. *I need to be inside you.*

Thank Jobin.

You may not say that in a minute. Denyan stood and grabbed some of the oil he had put on his body before he went onstage. Flipping up the cap, he poured some into his palm and, after liberally coating his cock, used the remainder on that tight little rosette. Throwing the tube within reach, he went to his knees behind Micah again. He took hold of his cock and placed it at the opening to Micah's body, just letting it sit there. Passing the crown through the firm pucker would be the most painful part, so he leaned forward and ran his hands over the hunter's back, gentling him, calming him, but he could still feel the tightness in his muscles.

Denyan?

Yeah?

Stick it in.

Prince Denyan couldn't help but chuckle at Micah's silent command. He'd been so worried about hurting him and all the man wanted was to feel him pushing his way inside. The prince was more than happy to comply.

Grabbing his cock with one hand, he gently pressed against the reluctant flesh. Micah cried out in pain, but Denyan continued to push. He kept a tight hold on his erection as he shoved, not stopping, even when Micah yelled as the puckered tissue swallowed the thick head.

Prince Denyan knew the pain seemed unbearable but also knew it would pass. Once the head was inside, the prince pressed further until his balls were sitting against Micah's flesh and he was all the way in.

Are you okay?

I'm not sure.

The prince was well aware that Micah was burning from the penetration, but he also knew the pain would recede to be replaced by pleasure.

Denyan put his hands on his lover's back and just let them rest there while he gave Micah time to adjust. He was able to study the hunter's body and see how graceful the lines of his back were. Although he was a big man, he was beautifully proportioned, muscular without being bulky, wide at the shoulders but slim in the waist and from this angle Denyan could see the marvelous shape of his torso as it dipped at the waist then flowed up to his tight butt. He was like a living work of art.

Prince Denyan smiled. The only thing this respite was accomplishing was to enlarge his rod even more. The longer his cock stayed clutched inside Micah's tight passage, the longer and thicker he got. He couldn't wait anymore.

I need to move. He put his hands on Micah's hips and pulled back a bit.

Micah cried out.

Am I hurting you?

Yes, but I want you to move. I want to know what it feels like when you move inside me.

Denyan needed no further encouragement. He gently pulled all the way back only to slide in again. Micah howled, but his lover showed him no quarter. Denyan looked down and watched his heavy cock disappear into Micah's body, the hunter's passage tightly clenching him. He moved his hands to Micah's back, feeling the strength coiled in that powerful body as he plied his shaft in and out with a steady rhythm.

"Do you like it when I slide in nice and slow like this?" Denyan asked as he gently swung his body back and forth.

Micah couldn't speak as he relished the prince's slow, delectable journey within his body.

"Ah, nothing to say," the prince said. "Perhaps you'd like it better if I pushed harder." And with that he moved his hands back to Micah's hips and used the leverage to slam into the bounty hunter. The small room was filled with that smack of flesh against flesh along with their whispered words.

Prince Denyan was sure he was hurting Micah, he was gripping him so tightly. But he needed to be anchored, physically and mentally, as he thrust into him. His balls tightened and he shot off, sending wave after wave of hot cum exploding into that welcoming channel.

It seemed to last forever.

The connection was incredible.

Prince Denyan slumped over Micah's back, turning his head to lay his cheek against the slick skin. He was having trouble catching his breath after detonating inside that slick passage. His lover hadn't had a chance to come, but he was definitely going to remedy that in a minute.

But it was Micah who broke the silence after a few seconds.

"Now it's my turn."

Chapter Nine

ꙮ

Micah's voice galvanized Denyan into action. He pulled his cock all the way out, feeling the hunter wince. Rising to his feet, Prince Denyan turned and grabbed a chair which he hauled over beside Micah. By this time he had also risen to his feet, curious to see what the prince had planned for them.

"Sit down," Denyan ordered.

Micah raised his eyebrows. "You have your cock inside me once and you think you can tell me what to do."

"I like to order you around. I suspect that not many people are willing to take you on, but I like the power it gives me. I also love the pleasure it gives me…and you. Now can you just sit in the damn chair?"

"And will you make it good for me?" the hunter laughed as he squirmed on the cold chair.

"Oh, I can guarantee that it will be good," Denyan threw back as he turned away from Micah and straddled his legs. "It'll be good for me, but probably better for you."

Micah swallowed hard as he took in the masculine beauty of Prince Denyan's body. "Put your hands on your thighs and back up so I can put my mouth on you," he commanded.

The prince seemed delighted to comply and placed his ass level with Micah's mouth so all he had to do was grab his hips and haul him back.

After just a second of hesitation, he stuck out his tongue and licked one of the prince's cheeks.

That initial touch of his tongue to Prince Denyan's flesh was like nothing he could have ever imagined. It tasted forbidden and dark, like night secrets, with a texture that was rough and so unlike the smooth skin of a woman. The scent was that of an aroused male, hard and powerful like Denyan himself, and Micah loved it.

He rubbed his hands up and around Prince Denyan's ass, following the contours of his body, finding the secret hollows and swells. His shaft hardened as he learned the form of this man. Using just his palms, he swept them across the prince's ass, reveling in the way the coarse hair tickled his skin. Then he moved to the crack and ran his thumbs slowly up and down the edge of the crease. When he realized that by making the prince wait he was punishing himself as well, he spread Denyan's cheeks wide to expose his place of pleasure.

Leaning forward, Micah prodded, feeling the puckered tightness with the point of his tongue and began to lick in earnest, voracious in his need to service the prince. He used his saliva to ease his way inside, finally replacing tongue with finger and gently drawing it in and out, readying him to take his huge cock.

Easing his finger out, he slapped the prince on the butt, saying, "Grab that lube."

Denyan stepped away and picked up the tube, turning to let Micah watch as he spread the lubricant over his opening. Micah looked down to see his own cock leaking drops of pre-cum, weeping in its need for the prince.

"I'll take that stuff when you're done with it," he said.

The prince squirted some of the oil into Micah's upturned hand and Micah took his cock and liberally coated it with the lubricant.

This time there was no conversation, no debate, no preamble. Denyan walked over to Micah, turned his back to the hunter and, as Micah held his throbbing erection for him, he slid it home.

They sat immobile, Denyan's body adjusting to the enormous invasion and Micah's body relishing the incredible feeling of being inside another man's body for the very first time. Then the prince used his hands to lift up from the hunter's cock and slide down.

If Micah had had any doubts or hesitations about making love with a man, they flew out the window the instant Denyan moved. He was able to run his hands down his muscular back as the prince levered himself up and down Micah's cock, sometimes rising and falling slowly, sometimes pressing down hard. And Micah loved it. Pushing his hips up let him answer the prince's downward slide with his own upward thrust. It was delicious—slide, thrust, slide, thrust, slide, thrust into that tight little hole.

But it wasn't enough.

Grabbing Denyan's waist, he jammed him down hard on his erection, feeling the prince using his powerful legs to push back up. But each time, Micah slammed him down again until their bodies were slick with sweat and takeoff was imminent. With just enough time to reach around and seize Denyan's cock in his fist, his own load shot off into the prince's body, gushing jets of cum into that snug channel.

With his hand on the prince's cock when he went off, Micah could feel it jerking and bucking as the load within came shooting out. Raw energy raced through his hand, through his body as he clutched the prince's cock through its release. All the hunter could do was slump forward, his head on Denyan's back. He felt the prince leaning back against him, too exhausted to remain upright.

That was when he felt her approaching.

"Get up," he said to Denyan, pushing the prince to his feet and rising to stand in front of him. He knew who was coming but had no idea what she was doing here.

Prince Denyan stood, confused by the complete turnaround in Micah. Gone was the lover, replaced by the hunter.

Micah wasn't surprised in the least when the lock deactivated and the door swung open. He put out his arm to keep the prince from stepping forward.

"I know who it is," he said, shaking his head in disbelief. *What is she doing here and how in Jobin's name did she escape the cuffs? And how did she deactivate the portal security?*

Then Layla stepped into the room. With the tight black breeches that hugged her body, along with knee-high leather boots, she looked like she'd stepped from some lucky man's wet dream. But the torso armor and the fearless expression on her face showed the fighter that she was.

"I'm not sure I want to know someone who can get past my entry security so easily," the prince smiled. "And then again, maybe I do," he added, sweeping her body with a slow perusal. Although he may have preferred his sex with men, he could still appreciate the beauty of a gorgeous woman like the one who had just entered his dressing chamber.

Despite the high level security, he thought.

"This is Layla. She's another bounty hunter from *The Renegade*," Micah said.

Even before Prince Denyan had a chance to speak, Layla started in on Micah. "You need to get dressed."

She raised her head and sniffed the air. "Geez, this room reeks of sex." she said to Micah as she threw his clothes at him. "Where's the prince?"

Neither of the men had a chance to answer.

"That's terrible," she ranted on as the two men quickly got dressed. "You're supposed to be checking on Prince Denyan and here you are fucking some gorgeous stud."

The prince threw his head back and roared with laughter.

"What's so funny?"

"Allow me to introduce myself. I'm not just a gorgeous stud, I'm also Prince Denyan."

Micah didn't think he'd ever seen anyone's face go as red as Layla's.

"You're the prince," she sputtered, looking him up and down. "I mean, I'm very sorry, Your Highness. Please accept my apologies for my rude behavior." Layla made a clumsy bow.

Grabbing Layla by the arm, Micah turned her to him and said, "What's going on and how in Jobin's name did you get out of those cuffs?"

"Cuffs?" Denyan said curiously.

"You keep out of this. I mean, please stay out of this, Your Highness," Layla said, bowing again amid her confusion.

Micah had the gall to laugh and that just made her angrier. She turned on him, saying, "It's lucky I did get out of them or I wouldn't be here to warn you."

"What do ya mean, 'warn me'? What's going on?"

"It took me a while to get free after you left." She heard the prince chuckle behind her and swung around to glare at him.

"Sorry," he said with a slight bow, which she acknowledged with one of her own.

"I really was going to stay behind just like you asked even though I could have easily followed you. I got dressed..." Denyan raised an eyebrow, but Layla ignored him. "And decided to go out for a bite to eat. I had just headed into the bathroom when the door to the main chamber blew apart."

Layla shook her head in annoyance "I was too busy fuming about being left behind to pick up the approaching Redelians."

"Redelians?" Micah asked.

"Yes, our information managers were wrong about that. I guess somehow the Redelians figured out what you're up to."

"I had no idea they were following me. Proves I've been spending too much time thinking about other things."

Despite her annoyance, Layla loved the pointed look he gave her. But it was a look that quickly changed to one of horror.

I left you there, handcuffed to the bed. You would have been at their mercy.

I was out of the cuffs long before they burst in.

Thank Jobin for that.

"I didn't know how many of them there were but there was only one of me and since they're seven feet tall with long, sharp claws, I decided to take the path of least resistance. As soon as I heard them smashing their way in, I climbed on the commode, pulled aside one of the ceiling baffles and crawled up into the space, setting the baffle back into place behind me. I could hear them tearing apart the room. I don't know if they were looking for you or for me, but they were mighty annoyed when they found the room empty." Layla shivered and Micah drew her into his arms and let her continue.

"They came into the bathroom, but when they found it empty, they turned and left. That's when I moved aside the ceiling tile just enough to confirm the identity of the intruders." She shivered again at just the thought of the creatures.

"And they were Redelians?" Micah asked.

Layla nodded against his chest.

"What would they be doing so far from their base planet?" Denyan asked. "They like to wage war close to home. That way they don't have far to transport their captives for slave labor."

Layla and Micah both swung around to look at him.

"What?" he said.

"They're looking for you," Micah explained.

"Me?" he asked incredulously. "Why would the Redelians be looking for me? I have no quarrel with them."

"You may not, but they think they have a quarrel with your father," Micah said.

"I don't understand. We have no dispute with the Redelians."

"Start at the beginning, Micah," Layla encouraged.

"Brachan, the leader of the Redelians, wanted Delia Monroe," Micah explained.

Prince Denyan frowned. "What does she have to do with any of this? She's a fighter pilot for the Wardelian League, isn't she?"

Micah nodded. "It's a convoluted story. Brachan hates Delia. She helped his wife escape Brachan's torture, so he forced your father to lure her to Tantor."

"What does Brachan want with Delia?"

"To punish her for interfering in his affairs. He lost face when she rescued his wife and, to the Redelians, that's a very serious matter. Brachan wants his wife back and only Delia knows where she is."

"How did he get my father to convince Delia to come to Tantor?" the prince asked.

"He took Princess Tresta."

"That bastard kidnapped my baby sister!" The prince took off for the door, as if he were going to rescue the princess. Micah grabbed his arm.

"It's all taken care of. Another bounty hunter has gone to bring her back. That's what we do."

"Do you think he'll be able to find her?"

"He's already on the way to meet with Brachan."

"Meet with Brachan," the prince scoffed.

"Actually, that's a euphemism for 'do whatever's necessary to find Princess Tresta and bring her back'."

"That I can live with. But I still don't understand what happened between my father and Brachan."

"When Princess Tresta was captured, your father went a bit crazy and involved the bounty hunters from *The Renegade*."

"You mean, he asked them for help?"

"Not exactly. He kidnapped Toryn, the ship's navigator from the star cruiser, drawing Jude Roland, the captain, into the picture."

"Great Jobin. What was he thinking?"

"He wasn't. The king told Jude that he would exchange Toryn for Delia. When Jude arrived with her, Brachan was waiting to take her."

Prince Denyan shook his head at Micah's incredible tale.

Micah continued. "Jude was able to rescue Toryn and trick the Redelian leader into letting Delia go. But nothing your father said would convince Brachan that he had no part in the plot. Now the king is afraid that the fiend may retaliate against his family."

Now Denyan was beginning to understand. "That's why you came. You're here to protect me," he said.

"Looks like he was doing more than protecting you," Layla said impishly.

This time it was Denyan's turn to glare.

Micah laughed. "It turns out the prince and I have a connection as well," he said to Layla.

"I thought he might be the one," she said.

"You think he's the final link in our circle of three?" Micah asked.

Before Layla could answer, she felt a change in the air around them.

"They're here," she whispered.

Knowing exactly who she meant, Micah said, "They must have followed you."

Layla just raised her eyebrows at him. "Is there a back way out of here?" she asked Denyan.

The prince pressed a button under the lip of his dressing table and the entire table and mirror swung out, revealing a concealed passageway.

"Go, go!" she called to Micah. "Get the prince out of here!"

"Don't be crazy!" he cried. "You take him."

She stood and looked right in his face. "Your mission is to protect the prince. Now do your job." She raised herself onto her tiptoes and kissed him full on the lips, then turned to face the door as blows began to rain on it.

Micah pushed the prince through the secret opening, taking one last look at Layla as she stood quietly waiting. The prince activated the closing mechanism and she was lost from sight.

From within the passage, Micah heard the door of the dressing chamber being blown open. He and Prince Denyan descended a set of steps and continued down a long tunnel, leaving Layla to face the Redelians alone.

ChapterTen

ॐ

Micah was almost sick with despair at abandoning Layla. He was well aware of what kind of creatures the Redelians were and that they would show her no mercy. He knew all about the ten-inch green prong they had between their legs and its razor-sharp barbs, meant to rip the victim apart on entry and withdrawal.

The poor unfortunates were hauled to Redelian renewalchambers to be healed immediately so the torment could begin anew until they would beg for death, for release. Micah was sure that Layla would never let them take her alive. She'd heard the stories as well.

As he and Denyan stumbled along the darkened tunnel, he still felt a tenuous connection with her, but the further they went, the fainter it became until it was completely extinguished. Micah had no idea whether that meant there was too great a distance between Layla and himself or if the Redelians had killed her. He was so busy with his thoughts that he didn't realize the prince had stopped and turned around until he walked into him.

"I think we should go back and help her," he said, trying to fight his way past Micah. "We can't just leave her at the mercy of those barbarians."

"You felt the breaking of the connection too, didn't you?" Micah said.

Denyan nodded and Micah knew that, even in the short time the prince had been with Layla, the link had begun to be revealed. The three of them had been meant to be together. Micah's heart ached. They'd only begun to explore their relationship, to find out about their connection, and now they would never know the joy found in being together as three.

He felt devastated.

How would they survive when the bond was incomplete? How would they survive without Layla?

With all his heart Micah wanted to say yes and go back and help her, but he knew he couldn't jeopardize the prince's life like that. He and Layla had chosen a dangerous profession, had entered it knowing full well the risks involved. Layla hadn't been a part of this mission, but she understood that he had a duty to fulfill and that duty was to protect the prince at all costs, even if it meant her life.

Eventually the tunnel led to a small grate in the pavement down an alley a few blocks from The Mandate. Micah pushed the grate aside and pulled himself out of the hole. He made Denyan wait until he had checked the area thoroughly, but there was no sign of anything but a small six-legged cat. He hauled the prince to the pavement and they walked slowly to the mouth of the alley where Micah hailed a speederform.

Everything seemed so normal around them. Vehicles soared by with no regard for anyone. People called to one another, yet Micah felt like part of himself had died.

The driver dropped them off at the same entry to the passageway leading to the dock where Micah had begun his journey. He couldn't believe what had happened in such a short time, how much he had lost. Almost immediately two transplatforms appeared and zipped them to the main landing bay and up to the tiny berth where Micah's pod was docked.

Micah stepped off the platform and right away began to pace the width of the little holding area, head down, fists clenched. Guilt welled up in him. "I shouldn't have left her to battle the Redelians alone. I should have stayed and fought."

Prince Denyan stepped in front of him and grabbed Micah by the shoulders. "What if it had been Jude?"

Micah's head shot up. "What?"

"What if the other bounty hunter had been Jude? Would you have hesitated to leave him to meet the Redelians alone?"

Micah hesitated. "I don't know."

"That's bullshit and you know it. If it had been Jude, you would have found it a lot easier to take me to safety and leave him to take care of the Redelians. Isn't that right?" He shook Micah. "Isn't that right?"

With a slow nod of his head, Micah stubbornly agreed. "I would have left him, but I wouldn't have wanted to. But you're right, it would have been easier with Jude."

Denyan put one hand gently on the side of Micah's face. "She's strong, she's well trained and she's certainly proven to be resourceful. Why don't we wait a while so she can catch up with us, then we'll all leave together."

Micah managed a thin smile. "That's a good idea. We wait a bit and when she gets here, we'll head back to *The Renegade*."

Half an hour later, he said nothing as only he and the prince climbed into the speeder pod. He set the coordinates to rendezvous with *The Renegade,* not even noticing when the little craft went in and out of *jergaspeed.*

* * * * *

Jude and Toryn were waiting with Delia when the little pod docked. Micah had already sent a message so, knowing about the loss of Layla, they said little as he and Denyan disembarked.

"I can show the prince to a chamber if you'd like to be alone," Delia said.

It was obvious from the way they looked at him that they were all aware of his connection to Layla. Micah knew these three bounty hunters above all others could understand what it must feel like to have a connection severed.

Micah turned to Denyan and drew him into his arms. "I need to be alone for a while," he said.

"Come to me when you're ready," the prince said. "I'll be waiting for you."

Prince Denyan stepped away from the comfort of Micah's embrace to follow Delia from the landing bay.

Jude put his hand on Micah's arm. "You did a good job keeping him safe, you know. That was your duty."

"Duty doesn't fill up the emptiness in my heart or the need in my soul," Micah said bleakly. "Duty won't give me back my soul mate."

Pulling away from Jude's grasp, Micah turned and left the landing bay.

* * * * *

Somehow Micah made his way to his cabin where he stripped off his clothes, dimming the bedside lamp before falling into bed. He lay there in the soft light, staring into the shadows of the room.

His heart fell like it had been torn in two. How could he go on without her? For years he'd thought there was no soul mate for him, no woman who was his other half. Instead he'd discovered that Jobin had blessed him with two such people, two lovers who shared a bond with him. A bond that now was broken, that would remain incomplete. For the first time in years, tears began to slip from his eyes. And he did nothing to stop them.

He remembered the first time he'd seen Layla when Jude had brought her on board *The Renegade*. After hearing the story of how she'd taken down Staar, he'd expected a seven-foot Jargoth. Instead he'd been introduced to a petite and very beautiful young woman who had turned her smile on him. He'd taken one look and knew he needed to stay away from her. Micah had wanted her instantly, with a raging, painful hard-on, but he was much too old for her.

He loved the way she'd wrested control of their lovemaking on Chend. And the way she'd just as eagerly let him take it back. Their connection had been so new and he'd been so stupid to think he could ignore it, ignore her.

She wouldn't be ignored. She'd proven that to him in the hotel room on S'Leng 3. In fact she'd proven it on the floor, on the bed and in the shower chamber. And now she was gone.

When Prince Denyan had struggled with him to go back and help her, he'd almost given in. But the mission had been to protect the prince and that was exactly what he'd done. He'd fulfilled his duty, but at what cost.

Exhaustion was claiming him, yet he was afraid to sleep, not sure whether he wanted to dream about Layla or escape to a dreamless slumber. If he dreamed of her, she would still be gone when he awoke, but maybe dreams were the only way he would be able to keep her close.

He woke up, knowing he would have to struggle to keep the tears at bay. She'd followed him into his dreams, laughing and loving him. But it was only an illusion. She wasn't here. Micah waited for the pain that would come with that admission.

But something had changed.

The grief was gone.

A woman stepped from the shadows near the bed. No light was needed to know who it was. Love flowed from her and washed over him, healing his grieving soul.

"Layla," he murmured. Moving to him, she stroked his face. He gently took her hand and placed a kiss on her palm, then joyously pulled her to him.

Gathering her in the circle of his arms, he held her tightly, unable to believe that she was safe. They lay for long minutes until Micah reached over and activated the bedside lamp.

"I need to see that you're really here, that you're all right." As Layla went to her knees beside him, Micah shifted so they were kneeling face to face.

He kissed her forehead, ran his hands down her arms, assuring himself that she was really there. It was then he noticed the cut above her eye and the layer of dirt covering her clothing and dusting her hair.

"What happened?" he cried. "I thought you were dead."

"Well, to tell you the truth when the door blew open, I thought that was it for me, but I tried not to panic. When the Redelians blew in the door, it threw up a cloud of dust, which gave me just enough time to try my old trick one more time."

"You climbed into the ceiling again, didn't you?" he asked.

"Yes, but it was more difficult with the layer of dust on everything. I was afraid they'd see my footprints on the dressing table where I'd stood to climb up into the space above the baffles."

"You were able to redirect their thoughts away from the table," he said with certainty, now seeing the extent of her abilities. "And that's why the connection between us faded. You couldn't maintain the two connections simultaneously."

"I had to make a choice and it turned out to be the right one. The Redelians are extraordinarily easy to play mind games with. They're a very physical race and although not stupid, they're susceptible to thought redirection. I'm sure they looked right at the footprints, but never even saw them."

"Remind me never to make you mad enough to try that out on me," Micah said.

"It would never work with you," she said, swatting his arm. "Your mind is much too strong for that. You'd always see the truth."

Micah's face grew serious. "When I thought you were gone, I did see the truth. I need both you and Prince Denyan in my life. I know now that we're connected with the same kind of bond that Jude and the others have."

A voice spoke from the doorway. "That's exactly what my vision showed," the prince said. "The three of us belong together."

"Prince Denyan," Layla cried. Getting off the bed, she went to him. The prince took her in his arms and held her close.

"I'm so glad you're safe," he murmured, gently tucking her head under his chin.

Micah joined them. "You knew she was here?"

"Only a few moments ago. It was the strangest thing. My body was surrounded by warmth until I felt the connection become whole again. I knew she must be with you."

Moving back a step, Layla looked at the prince. "I had great incentive to keep myself out of the clutches of the Redelians and get back to the two of you."

"What do you mean?" Prince Denyan asked.

"You were talking about your visions. Did they show *you* what mine showed *me*? That we won't just be working together?"

"If you mean the three of us being lovers, then yes, I saw that too," the prince replied.

"Good. Then you two'd better get your clothes off," she said with a laugh. She saw Denyan hesitate. "What's the matter? Are you too shy?" Then Layla grew serious. "I'm sorry. Maybe you don't want to make love with a woman."

"I'm not shy at all," he replied. "And I most definitely want to make love with you, with you and Micah." He looked down at her clothes that were covered in dust. "But maybe you'd like to shower first. I don't really mind making love with a dusty woman, but I'm pretty intrigued by the thought of trying out *The Renegade*'s famous shower chamber, with you two. I just met Jude in the corridor and he told me how glad he was that you were okay. He also happened to mention that the shower chamber is available for the three of us to use."

Layla looked down at her grubby clothes as if seeing them for the first time and laughed. "I was so glad to escape the Redelians and get back to the ship that I never even noticed how dirty I was. After hearing all the stories, I'd love to try out the shower chamber and I'll be even happier to get into some clean clothes."

"Not as happy as we'll be to get you out of those filthy ones. Right Micah?" the prince said grinning.

He turned as Micah made no reply. Micah was standing looking at Layla with a puzzled expression on his face.

"What's the matter?" Layla asked following Denyan's gaze.

"Well, I see how you got away from the Redelians, but I haven't figured out how you got to *The Renegade*. How did you get back here?" Micah asked.

"After you two left, the Redelians methodically tore the dressing room apart, but they just couldn't seem to figure out how you had escaped."

Micah smiled at her. "No wonder you couldn't keep our connection."

Layla shrugged as if trying to brush off the severity of the whole affair. "I couldn't keep them from looking. I don't have that kind of mental ability. But I was able to plant the idea that they completely ignore the dressing table and they seemed to accept that suggestion quite easily."

"But how did you get back here?" This time it was Denyan who spoke.

"After the Redelians had assured themselves that there was no one there and the room had no secret exits, they just walked through the debris of what was left of the door and stormed out. I waited until I was sure it was safe, then I moved the ceiling baffle aside and climbed down. I made my way through the wreckage, opened the secret door and went down into the tunnel. I stumbled along in the dark for quite a while before I came to the grate that opened into the alley."

Turning to look at Prince Denyan, she grinned. "I'm afraid you'll have to do some remodeling before your dressing room can be used again."

"I doubt if I'll be going back to Kingoolia. I think my stint on S'Leng 3 has come to an end," the prince said.

Micah drew Layla into his arms. "We waited for you at the landing bay, but when you didn't come, we assumed the worst."

"I had to wait while the Redelians did a thorough search and destruction of the room and it was a long haul through the pitch-black tunnel. I tried to connect with you, but you were too far away."

"We don't want to lose you. Not so soon after the three of us have found each other. Finish your story," he said gently, nuzzling the top of her head with his lips.

Stepping back from the warmth of Micah's body, Layla continued the tale. "There's not really much left to tell.

"I took a speederform that dropped me back at the entry to the tunnel that led to the landing bay. When the transplatform left me off in the landing bay, I just looked around until I was able to find a way back to *The Renegade,* then..."

"She means she lifted some sort of craft when nobody was looking," Micah clarified to Denyan.

Denyan laughed. Layla glared.

"I'm sure no one even noticed it was gone. When I got here, I just reprogrammed its coordinates and sent it straight back to the same holding bay where I'd found it. So even if I did borrow it without permission, I did return it."

"How in Jobin's name did you manage to steal..."

"Borrow," Layla interjected.

"How in Jobin's name did you manage to st...I mean, borrow a craft? All vessels are locked to allow use only by the pilot or authorized personnel," Prince Denyan said, shaking his head in disbelief.

"Let's just say that locking your door won't keep her out," said Micah with a laugh."

Layla, who was getting a bit uncomfortable with the direction the conversation was taking, spoke up. "I really need to get cleaned up. Is anybody else planning to shower or am I going to be trying out the wonderful shower chamber all by myself?"

As Micah scooped Layla up in his arms, he turned to the prince. "Come on. I happen to know that Jude's shower chamber is more than big enough for three."

Chapter Eleven

ꟹ

"I certainly am glad the captain's cabin is so close. It's lucky we didn't bump into anyone with you wandering around the ship in the raw," Layla said, laughing as Micah set her down inside the doorway of the bathchamber.

"I guess that would be their problem. I couldn't wait to get in here and get the two of you naked," was Micah's reply.

Layla stared around the opulent room. Her eyes flew open in amazement at her first look at the captain's shower chamber. "Big enough for three? It looks big enough for ten," Layla said, surveying the shower area.

"I wonder how you use all those multilevel seats." Denyan mused, coming to stand beside her.

"And what are all those different showerheads for? And how come they're all at different heights?" Layla wondered aloud.

"And how do you get them to work?" Prince Denyan asked.

Micah was already opening the door to the shower chamber. "Jude was talking about it one day and said you just need to call out your commands and everything will work automatically. It's programmed that way. Did you notice that even the floor of the bathchamber is heated? That's Toryn's genius at work as well. He loves to tinker."

Layla quickly stripped off her clothes and joined Micah. They both turned to see what was keeping Denyan. "What are you waiting for?" Micah asked.

"I finally get to be part of one of my visions and I intend to savor every moment of it. I was enjoying just watching the two of you." He began to take off his clothes, revealing his beautiful body little by little to Micah and Layla.

"Stop teasing us," Layla said.

Prince Denyan laughed and took his time getting out of his shirt and breeches. He loved the hungry looks that Micah and Layla threw him.

When he finally stepped into the shower chamber, he took Layla into his arms, while Micah cradled her from the back.

"I'm so glad that you're safe. I could feel Micah's pain when we thought we'd lost you."

"I'm so sorry I couldn't let you both know that I was all right, but I needed all my energy to keep the Redelians distracted. Well, I'm safe and now I'd really like to get the dust off me. Anybody want to help?"

"I'll see if I can get this high showerhead to come on," the prince said, turning away. "Number Two, on."

Layla started to giggle as a thin spray shot out from a low nozzle instead of from the one Denyan wanted. Then she realized exactly where the spray would hit her.

"Oh, I'd like to try that one once I'm all clean," she said, a bit breathless.

"I'll help you," Prince Denyan offered. Layla laughed and swatted his arm.

"Let me see what I can do," Micah said. "Number Two, off. Number Three, on." The low spray shut off immediately and two small doors slid up to reveal hidden recesses.

"Ah, Number Three opens secret compartments. What's in there?" Layla asked, trying to peer inside.

Micah reached in and grabbed something.

Prince Denyan looked over Layla's shoulder. "What is it?"

Micah held out his hand. "Oh, some lube," the prince said, with a wide grin. "That oughtta come in handy. Set it down on one of those seats."

"My turn now," Layla announced. "I'm going to be logical. Number One, on." She whooped with delight when the tallest showerhead came on.

Micah smiled and said, "And I found the soap."

He had pushed his hand into the other slot in the wall and come out with a generous dollop. Rubbing it into a lather, he began to slide his hands over Layla's back. Down that graceful spine and up, along her sculpted shoulders, down her slender arms, he blazed a slippery trail. It was a trail that ended at the cheeks of her ass, with a slick finger slipping down her crease, entering her channel ever so gently.

But she was being pleasure-tortured by them both. Prince Denyan had also slid his hand into the slot, taking some soap, now caressing her luscious breasts, playing with her nipples. She arched her back, pressing her breasts into his hands, pushing her ass back to Micah. Denyan smoothed his hand down her body, between her legs, seeking her sensitive clit. Gentle circles, then back and forth, looking to find what pleased her.

Micah snatched up the lube and smoothed it over his ready cock. "I'm going to slide into you nice and slow," he whispered. "But first, why don't we let Denyan sit down and get comfortable. I suspect that if he sat right there, "Micah pointed to the raised seat at the end of the shower chamber, "you could take him in your mouth at the same time."

The prince backed up and, using the vertical bars on either side, pulled himself up onto the shower seat and set his feet into the footholds in the wall.

As Layla stepped forward and took the prince in her mouth, Micah slid inside her, setting a leisurely rhythm which she matched on Denyan's rod. When he began to push harder, go deeper, he took her by the waist so she could put her hand on Denyan's erection, anchoring it while she slid her mouth up and down.

Prince Denyan sighed in sheer bliss as Layla's warm mouth pleasured his cock. He put his hands to her elegant back, tenderly tracing over her silky skin, relishing the delights of making love with a woman, their softer ways, their knowing touch.

The prince looked down at her, now running her tongue under the collar of his massive erection, moaning as she put only the crown in her mouth to suck and lick at it. The whole picture was so erotic, to be emblazoned in his brain forever. Micah thrusting into her from behind, the sight of her tongue sleeking over his cock, the rise and fall of her head as she moved up and down his shaft.

His whole body shivered in sheer delight. Balls drawing back, breathing growing sharper, head of his cock expanding, sending out that first telltale weeping of pre-cum. A second of motionlessness, then he shot a stream of juice down her throat, pumping her mouth until there was nothing left. Spent, he shut his eyes and listened to Micah and his provocative words to Layla.

"You are so beautiful," Micah murmured. "I love to look down and see my cock disappearing into your body. When I slide back out, it's covered in your juice. I can see it all shiny from being inside you. Denyan, come and look at this."

Layla moaned at his sexy words.

But Prince Denyan didn't look. Instead he slid from the shower seat and grabbed the lube, for Micah's tight opening. One finger slipped inside and rubbed along the top of his inner channel. The prince knew exactly what that felt like. He knew that Micah's already tightly wound body would be spiraling toward completion.

"Oh great Jobin," Micah cried. "I don't think I can stand that while I'm inside her." Denyan smoothed his finger along the sensitive inner flesh again and again.

"Of course you can stand it. You love it. Don't you?" No answer. "Tell me you love it," he commanded. With one hand on Micah's back, he could feel the warrior's muscles shifting and bunching as he swung in and out of Layla's body. The other hand caught the first pulsings of the tiny gland just inside the constricted opening. "Tell me you love it," he commanded again.

Instead of answering, Micah went off like a star cruiser hitting *jergaspeed.* Denyan could feel the contractions pulsing around his finger, as he jetted his release.

He smiled, as Micah's first coherent thought was for Layla.

"Poor baby, you didn't finish yet, did you?" Micah whispered to her. "We'll just have to help you."

Prince Denyan drew out his finger and went to kneel at her feet. "I can help by putting my tongue right here." He demonstrated by touching her clit with his finger. "Oh, you're so swollen and ready. I bet you'll be absolutely delicious."

Denyan leaned forward to taste for himself and with Micah's cock still inside, the two lovers sent her off into ecstasy.

She howled her release, Micah moaning as she clutched his rod with her inner passage and Denyan lapping her rich cream as it wept from her body. All of her bones seemed to melt. Micah put his arms around her, to keep her from falling to the floor.

Denyan rose to his feet. "Bring her here, Micah. I'm sure she'd like to get under the spray."

Like a sleepwalker, Layla was propelled forward under the stream of water. Raising her head to let the water flow over her face, she breathed, "That was the most intense sexual experience I've ever had."

"And we've only gotten started," Micah said, in a silky, stroke-your-skin voice.

He and the prince got soap from the slot and gently washed Layla, showing with their tender caresses how thankful they were to have her back with them.

"Number Three, off," Micah called.

"Now that you're squeaky clean, let's play," he said, lifting Layla up and setting her on one of the higher level seats in the shower chamber. The seat was cut deep and high into the wall, so she could sit well back with two small vertical bars on each side to hold onto. "Put your hands on those bars and open your legs nice and wide."

Layla was more than eager to comply, leaving her body open almost at eye level.

"Look how beautiful she is here, Denyan," he said as he spread her full labia apart. "I love all the colors and textures of a woman's body here between her legs. Why don't you lick her there and see if she tastes as good as she looks?"

"Oh, I already know that, but I could never get enough."

The prince bent his head to take her plump lips in his mouth, sucking them hard and licking up the very center to penetrate under her little hood with the point of his tongue. He heard Layla cry out at he stabbed at her clit, pressing to make her squirm. Taking the hood in his mouth, he flattened it with his lips and tongue and pulled it away from her body.

"It sounds like someone eating a *fresshia*," Micah said from behind him.

"She's much more succulent and delicious than any galactic fruit I've ever tasted," Denyan said as he released her lips from his mouth, only to take his forefinger and gently insert it in her channel. He had just begun to move in and out of her when he heard the click of a tube being opened and felt Micah's hand on his ass.

"Thank Jobin we found the lube," Micah said as he ran his now-slick middle finger up and down the crease of Denyan's ass, preparing him. "I just put some on this hard-on of mine, so why don't you put your mouth back on that gorgeous slit and I'll slide right inside you."

As the prince resumed his pleasuring of Layla, Micah took hold of his own stiff cock, set it at Denyan's snug opening and pushed in slowly. The enormous head pressed against the puckered flesh, forcing it to give way and the rest of his rod slid right in.

"You...feel...so...good," Micah said, each word emphasized by an unhurried stroke of his shaft. As he made the long measured swings back and forth, he relished the sound of Denyan pushing Layla toward her release. He was able to hold one hand on the prince's long sculpted back and the other on his hip, giving him leverage and also a nice unimpeded view of his own cock as it moved in and out of Prince Denyan's hole.

As Layla gripped the bars more tightly and pressed harder against the prince's mouth, Micah knew that Denyan had pushed her to the limit. She was ready to come, so he began to stroke quicker and deeper, hoping to force the prince to go off with her. Then it all began to jumble inside him as the erotic sound of Prince Denyan's quest for satisfaction was joined by Layla's frenzied moans.

Micah's whole body stiffened, signaling his own orgasm and he was taken by surprise as he shot off first, not able to wait for the other two. He filled Denyan's inner channel with his hot cum, pumping into him. He could only stand unmoving as Layla's keening cry mixed with the prince's bellow in the massive shower chamber. The room echoed with the panting of the three lovers as they tried to gain their breath.

Micah was the first to move, turning back to the high-level showerhead and calling it on, wetting his powerful body. Denyan swung around and stood between Layla's spread legs. Letting her wrap her legs around his waist, pressing her hot center against him, flattening her labia against his back so he could feel how slick she still was from his mouth.

"I don't know if I want to let him shower without me," Layla remarked, placing a hand on Prince Denyan's shoulder.

"Without us," the prince clarified.

As the two of them watched hungrily, their lover lathered his hands and smoothed them over his muscled chest.

Micah snorted when Layla continued, "You're so absolutely beautiful, Micah."

"This body is a bit too old to be called beautiful," he said, laughing, but he did take his hands and run them over his belly, teasing his audience.

Denyan leaned back against Layla, feeling her cream against his skin. "Judging by how wet she is, I'd say she doesn't find you old at all." He took in the hard body, the water running in rivulets through the soapy lather. "And neither do I. You've been in my visions for years and I've got to tell you that the flesh and blood man is much better than the one in my dream."

By now Micah had moved his hands further south and was washing his cock.

"Help me down, Denyan," Layla cried. "I want to do that."

Prince Denyan turned and, placing his hands at her waist, set her down on the floor of the shower chamber. Layla went to Micah and shoved his hands out of the way.

"Let me do that," she ordered, thrusting her hands into the soap recess and coating them.

"Everyone wants to order me around," he said, shaking his head.

"That's because we only get a chance to do it when we're making love with you," Layla quipped. Denyan nodded agreement.

"I'm not that hard to get along with, am I?" he asked in mock innocence.

Layla laughed. "We really like it when you're hard."

Micah moaned as Layla put her soapy hands on his cock, tugging it, running her hands around the head. His breath came in sharp pants as she massaged his balls with one slick hand while she tortured his cock with the other.

Looking down at his hard-on, Micah observed, "I guess I'm not as old as I thought."

Turning Layla, he placed her hands flat on the wall of the shower chamber, his hands on her waist, and slid into her from behind. Out of the corner of his eye, Micah saw the prince pick up the lube and the next thing he knew, Denyan's heavy cock was pushing its way inside him as he slid in and out of Layla.

They laughed as they struggled initially to find a rhythm that would work for three, but the atmosphere quickly changed as their connection set them in a common tempo of pleasuring.

Micah was in the middle, his cock inside Layla, Denyan's cock inside him. As he stroked into her tight, slick channel, Prince Denyan mirrored the movement in Micah's body. Putting one hand on the wall above Layla's, Micah slid the other down her belly, to her clit. Layla whimpered as Micah touched her clitoris. One finger under the hood, pulling it forward, stretching it, squeezing it between thumb and finger, while his cock filled her.

Prince Denyan bent forward, placing a line of kisses across Micah's shoulder blades. He savored the rhythm of three, the intricate triple dance of love. Smoothing his hands around Micah's torso, he took his nipples and pulled them. He liked how Micah moaned.

This time, being double-pleasured sent Layla off first, triggering spasms of delight that gripped Micah's rod deep inside her.

With the combined bliss of the two cocks, one giving and one getting, Micah didn't stand a chance and shot his release into Layla's welcoming body. Prince Denyan yelled as Micah's channel took the force of his unleashing.

"Number Three, off," Micah whispered.

* * * * *

Later as they lay together in Micah's bed, Layla mused. "I think I really like Number One."

Micah sucked in a breath as he remembered the force of the spray as it cleansed him of Denyan's cum.

Prince Denyan smiled, recalling how he'd helped Layla use it after their love-making. Unfortunately, Micah broke in on his thoughts.

"Denyan, if you're not going back to S'Leng 3, what are you going to do?"

"I haven't figured that out," he said languidly. "I'll think about it later."

"I want you to think about it now," Micah said. "I want you to think about coming to work on *The Renegade*."

"Doing what?"

"Being a bounty hunter. You could get implants like the other hunters and Layla and I could train you to fight. With the connection between the three of us, we'd be unbeatable."

Prince Denyan lay there, thinking about his two lovers. He couldn't imagine what he had done to deserve all this. He'd be able to be with Layla and Micah, for work and for play.

"Well, will you stay with us?" Micah asked.

"You already know the answer to that," Denyan said. "You and Layla and I belong together. Of course I'll stay."

Micah thought about his conversation with Delia.

Then I realized how much I envied what the three of you have, the closeness that flows into the way you work together, the way you hunt together. I realized that I wanted to be part of something like that. I want the same kind of trust that you have in each other.

He looked at his two lovers and knew that was what he had with them, that same bond of absolute trust.

Also by Kaenar Langford

Lucifer's Angel

About the Author

Although born in Ireland, Kaenar Langford lives north of Toronto in rural Ontario but that doesn't stop her from traveling the world in her mind and in her books. The love of romance and the exotic as well as a sense of humour are all entwined to produce stories that will seduce you and make you laugh.

Her husband and two sons have grown used to seeing only the back of her head as she is transported to wherever the writing takes her. She has become immune to the teasing of her colleagues who are delighted with her publication of Lucifer's Angel, her first novel.

Kaenar enjoys playing music and reading and has taken up the Scottish small pipes in the last few years. Of course, Irish music is what she loves to play. Being asked to publish with Ellora's Cave ranks right up there with the best things to ever happen to her.

Kaenar welcomes comments from readers. You can find her website and email address on her author bio page at www.ellorascave.com.

Tell Us What You Think

We appreciate hearing reader opinions about our books. You can email us at Comments@EllorasCave.com.

Why an electronic book?

We live in the Information Age—an exciting time in the history of human civilization, in which technology rules supreme and continues to progress in leaps and bounds every minute of every day. For a multitude of reasons, more and more avid literary fans are opting to purchase e-books instead of paper books. The question from those not yet initiated into the world of electronic reading is simply: *Why?*

1. ***Price.*** An electronic title at Ellora's Cave Publishing and Cerridwen Press runs anywhere from 40% to 75% less than the cover price of the exact same title in paperback format. Why? Basic mathematics and cost. It is less expensive to publish an e-book (no paper and printing, no warehousing and shipping) than it is to publish a paperback, so the savings are passed along to the consumer.
2. ***Space.*** Running out of room in your house for your books? That is one worry you will never have with electronic books. For a low one-time cost, you can purchase a handheld device specifically designed for e-reading. Many e-readers have large, convenient screens for viewing. Better yet, hundreds of titles can be stored within your new library—on a single microchip. There are a variety of e-readers from different manufacturers. You can also read e-books on your PC or laptop computer. (Please note that Ellora's Cave does not endorse any specific brands.

You can check our websites at www.ellorascave.com or www.cerridwenpress.com for information we make available to new consumers.)

3. ***Mobility***. Because your new e-library consists of only a microchip within a small, easily transportable e-reader, your entire cache of books can be taken with you wherever you go.
4. ***Personal Viewing Preferences.*** Are the words you are currently reading too small? Too large? Too... ANNOYING? Paperback books cannot be modified according to personal preferences, but e-books can.
5. ***Instant Gratification.*** Is it the middle of the night and all the bookstores near you are closed? Are you tired of waiting days, sometimes weeks, for bookstores to ship the novels you bought? Ellora's Cave Publishing sells instantaneous downloads twenty-four hours a day, seven days a week, every day of the year. Our webstore is never closed. Our e-book delivery system is 100% automated, meaning your order is filled as soon as you pay for it.

Those are a few of the top reasons why electronic books are replacing paperbacks for many avid readers.

As always, Ellora's Cave and Cerridwen Press welcome your questions and comments. We invite you to email us at Comments@ellorascave.com or write to us directly at Ellora's Cave Publishing Inc., 1056 Home Avenue, Akron, OH 44310-3502.

Cerridwen, the Celtic Goddess of wisdom, was the muse who brought inspiration to storytellers and those in the creative arts. Cerridwen Press encompasses the best and most innovative stories in all genres of today's fiction. Visit our site and discover the newest titles by talented authors who still get inspired - much like the ancient storytellers did, once upon a time.

ELLORA'S CAVE
ROMANTICA PUBLISHING

Lightning Source UK Ltd.
Milton Keynes UK
04 April 2011

170370UK00001B/25/P